TOUCHING FIFTY

A Novel

ANTHONY MCDONALD

Anchor Mill Publishing

Anchor Mill Publishing

4/04 Anchor Mill

Paisley PA1 1JR

SCOTLAND

anchormillpublishing@gmail.com

Cover design by Barry Creasy

For Stephen Gee with all my love.

But also in memory of Tony Linford.

Y, con mucho cariño, para N.D.F.

ONE

I walked into the welcoming brightness of The Harrow and sat down on one of the high stools at the bar. Outside the dusk of an early March evening was blanketing the fields and copses but in here the wood-burning stove burned a cheerful red. A few people I knew slightly were perched around the bar and I gave them a nod or a hallo according to the degree of slightness of our acquaintanceship. The stool next to mine was empty, but the one beyond it was occupied by a man I liked the look of. I only saw his profile, though. When I came in and sat down and was greeted by the barmaid he did not look up. I was disappointedly conscious of that.

I ordered a pint of Hophead and watched it being pulled, golden and lightly frothy, into a straight glass. The man I liked the look of took no notice of this. He was studiously playing with his phone. Then he broke off to order some tapas across the bar. Smoked pigeon breast, whitebait, and herring roe. I got my own phone out and pretended to be busy with it too.

He was lean and tall – so far as I could tell, since he was sitting down – and he had a straight nose and a firm chin. Dark hair, almost black. A few grey threads in it only – unlike in mine: my barnet is a mixture now of pepper and salt. A little younger than my fifty-one, I thought. Perhaps by two or three years.

I finished my pint unhurriedly and, unhurriedly too, he finished his. He ate his tapas, handed the plates back across the counter, and said he'd enjoyed them. I ordered another pint for myself, and so did he. But still he didn't look at me.

Francis the landlord materialised behind the bar. 'How's your hand?' he asked me.

'It's going great,' I told him. I placed it on the bar for his inspection, and wiggled the fingers at him to show that I could.

The man two stools to my left, the chap I'd been surreptitiously looking at, turned towards me suddenly. His eyebrows were strikingly black and his eyes looked much the same. There was a spark in each of them that, in the shock of this first encounter with them, looked like the diamond light of coal. 'What did you do to it?' he asked. His voice was friendly and concerned.

'I had a minor op,' I said, pushing the hand – it was my left one, and so for him the nearer one – along the bar towards him.

To my surprise he touched it, and fingered the scar. 'Carpal tunnel?' he asked.

'No,' I said. 'Dupuytren's contracture.'

He frowned. I explained a bit and then he nodded slowly, gravely. 'Oh yes,' he said. 'I know people with that.'

We got talking. We introduced ourselves. 'I'm Peter,' I said.

He chuckled at that. He said, 'I'm Paul.' We shook hands.

What did he do? Building work, he said. Property maintenance. Um – he owned a few houses too. Rented them out.

Made some money then, I thought.

And me? I shuffled on my stool. 'Bit of a portfolio,' I said. 'I do a bit of work in medical training. Role-play stuff.' I did a self-deprecating sort of shuffle of my face. 'I used to be an actor once. I work behind the bar in a pub not far from here...' I gestured vaguely towards the west. 'The King Billy.' He nodded. He knew it, of course. I went on, 'And the other thing is, I write.'

He pricked up his ears at that. They were small ears and looked good; they suited him. 'What sort of thing?'

'Freelance,' I said. 'Magazine articles and stuff.

Things for websites.' I looked away across the bar. 'Mostly things about being gay.' He nodded. Not too fast, not too slow. I saw that from the corner of my eye. 'I'm gay,' I said.

'Oh, OK,' he said, and snickered. 'I'm not, as it happens, but never mind.' I reckoned that was as near to saying, 'I like you,' as one male, of whatever sexual orientation, ever comes when talking to another.

We sat in silence for a minute or so, staring straight ahead of us in parallel gaze, carefully not glancing sideways at each other. Then Paul said, 'Um, do you mind me asking … do you have…?'

'A partner,' I helped him out. 'I did have. He died a year ago.'

'I'm sorry,' Paul said.

I wasn't going to go down the autobiographical route, or the sentimental one. 'You?' I asked brusquely. 'Partner-front, I mean.'

'We split up at Christmas,' he said.

'Oh,' I said. Caught out. 'I'm sorry.' I heard my voice grow gentle as I asked, 'How long?'

'How long together?'

I nodded.

'Twenty years.' Then his voice too became gentle as he asked me, 'How long for you?'

'Ditto,' I said. 'And now?' I went on. 'Are you...?' I didn't know what verb to choose, so I stopped.

'I'm on a couple of dating websites,' he said. He shrugged. 'Some interesting things.'

'Yeah,' I said. I wasn't going to ask if he'd just been looking, or chatting, or had got further than that.

'You too, I guess,' Paul said, half-turning away from me and now looking straight ahead of him.

'Haven't done the website thing,' I said. 'Not yet. I do OK meeting blokes in bars in London.'

Paul took a gulp of beer. 'Yeah, I understand.' He nodded. The nod told me he didn't want more information. But he did continue. 'It does seem easier for you lot. You like the look of each other and – pardon me – bang.' I laughed. 'While for the rest of us it's dinner, phone-calls and...'

'I know,' I said. 'You're right. For us the easy things are easier.'

He nodded an experienced nod. 'Sex, you mean.'

'Like I said. But the difficult things – the big things – are just as difficult.'

He swung round on his stool suddenly. His whole body this time, so that his splayed thighs and his crotch seemed to yawn towards me. His coal-black eyes flashed into mine. He didn't smile. He said earnestly, 'You mean love.'

'Um…' I said. I thought very fast for half a second. 'Yes, I did mean that. But in a general way. There's nothing at the moment that…'

'Yeah, yeah,' he said sympathetically. 'Time…'

I liked his economical way with words. 'Yeah,' I said. 'Time.' I took a swig of my beer.

Half a minute passed. Like in a pressure-cooker, a lot went on in that time. It was I whose whistle valve blew first. 'I'm seeing someone,' I said.

Paul smiled. 'Good for you.' A second's pause, then, 'Tell me about him.'

'He's Portuguese,' I said. 'Lives in London. Speaks perfect English. Smokes too much.' I shrugged. 'We're not in love or anything. He's a bus driver. We've met twice.'

'Sounds a good start,' Paul said. 'Guy who can drive… Head start over one that can't.' He began to worry about what he'd just said. That was on his face. 'Not that I'm into guys.' How quickly the moment arrived when straight guys found the need to say this.

'I know that,' I said, to reassure him. 'He's coming down in a couple of days,' I said. 'First time we'll be spending time together.'

'Staying how long?' Paul asked.

'Two days. That's as much time as he can get off.'

'What are you planning to do with him?'

'He already knows the area. Rye, Hastings. Thanks to a previous boyfriend. I thought I'd take him to Calais for the day.'

'Calais?' Paul laughed. 'You sure know how to spoil a guy. Why not take him to Bruges or somewhere a bit nice?'

'I know,' I said. 'But he's only here for forty-eight hours, and it'd take most of that to get to Bruges and back. And part of the point of getting him down here is to spend some time in bed together. Spending it all on boats, in cars and trains…'

'Sure,' said Paul, nodding again. 'Defeats the object.' Then he paused and seemed to peer very sharply into my face, as though he was planning to draw it at some future date. That or trying to read my thoughts perhaps… But it was neither of those things, it turned out. He said suddenly, 'We've met before. Well, sort of met. The night my girlfriend and I split up we went to the King Billy. You served our drinks. Then you brought our food to the table.'

'Oh gosh,' I said. It seemed a very unlucky coincidence to be looking back on. That our first meeting had occurred on, for him, a very bad day. I found I had no memory of him or that first meeting. Which surprised me, as I now thought him very nice-looking. I had to wonder whether that evening had begun happily, and they had rowed at some later point in the evening – after the dinner I'd served them – or whether they had already agreed to part, and were eating a solemn farewell meal to mark the occasion. I wasn't going to ask him. Neither scenario was a cheerful one to contemplate.

'Not quite sure what to say,' I said, with a nervous chuckle. 'That was a bit of an ill-starred moment for a first meeting. And actually, I don't remember it at all.' I did a pantomime gulp. 'Sorry. Now I've probably wounded your vanity.'

Paul said in an even tone, 'Why would you remember? It was a day like any other for you. Whereas for us…'

'Yes, of course,' I said. 'Obvious really.'

A little twisted smile appeared on his face. The kind of smile that I can only manage to describe as rueful. 'Let me get you another pint,' he said.

I let him.

We talked quite freely then. We were on our third pint now, and that always helps. We talked about different places we'd lived in. Paul had spent some time working in Australia when he was younger. I hadn't been so far afield, but I'd lived for a few years in Paris. Those two destinations, so very different, gave us plenty of conversational ammunition. Enough to last out that third pint, at least. But we found we had even more to say than that. We got into deeper stuff. Talked about the long-term relationships we'd both had, and had both lost. Talked about other relationships: ones that pre-dated those. Paul had been married for a time. When he was in his twenties. It had been a bit of a mistake for both of them, he said. Four years they'd lasted, but that was it. 'I'm sorry,' I said.

I had to think a bit when we reached the bottom inch of our pints. We'd been matching our speed of consumption, half consciously, half by a sort of instinct, in the way that every social drinker is familiar with. The next shout would be mine. If I didn't make the offer... We might never meet again. He would remember me as the guy he bought a beer for but who never returned the gesture; people always do remember that. But a fourth pint? We might get drunker than we wanted to get. The conversational waters might grow deeper than we really wanted them to... I decided to risk it. 'Let me get one more,' I said.

He offered no show of reluctance but accepted, just as I had done twenty minutes earlier, with a quiet, pleased-sounding, 'Thank you.' And a handsome smile.

I ordered some tapas for myself. A last-ditch bid for self-preservation in the face of this new onslaught of beer. Patatas bravas, whitebait, olives and bread. We talked now about the difference between living with someone and living without them. About the business of paying all the bills, of doing all the cooking, all the ironing and all the washing-up. We talked about something else, though we didn't say the word; we tiptoed round it. But it was there between us, hovering in the air between our two faces, between our two chests, between our two pairs of legs that were spread wide, facing each other across the gap between the bar stools… We were talking about loneliness.

'And this time of year,' I heard Paul say. 'You notice it, don't you. Having to put that extra blanket on that you never had to before.'

'Yes,' I said. 'Sometimes I have to get out of bed and put one on in the middle of the night.'

Paul nodded very gravely in sympathy with that. I realised that he had to do the exact same thing. 'It's tough, isn't it.'

My mind did one of those lurches that happen sometimes in the middle of the fourth pint. It was as if I'd bumped against a door and seen it open onto a possibility that a moment earlier I hadn't guessed was there. I saw the two of us going home together. His place or mine, it hardly mattered which. I saw the evening ending with the two of us naked and warming each other by cuddling in a large bed.

It took an almost physical effort to will that scenario away. It had to be resisted, even as something to be thought about. Straight men did go to bed with gay ones sometimes – I knew that from my own experience. But how they hated themselves the next morning! Paul wouldn't be going to bed with me; I had to make sure that he didn't suddenly, drunkenly propose it. It wasn't simply a question of Paul hating himself in the morning; he would wake up, I well knew, also hating me.

I drained my glass a little quickly and stood up. 'Well, I've had more than I meant to,' I said. 'And I have to drive home.'

Paul downed the last of his beer too. 'Ditto,' he said. 'Must go, as they say in Russia.' (He pronounced *must go* as *Moscow*.) He got down from his stool and we stood facing each other, swaying ever so slightly. Standing, he was about three inches taller than me. That made him about six foot one, I reckoned. 'It was nice talking to you,' he said.

'Really lovely to meet you,' I answered. Then I patted him on one shoulder twice, and he patted my shoulder, though just once, and then I turned quickly away, saying, 'See you again some time,' as I headed away to the door that led to the car-park, not looking back to see if he was following me or not. I unlocked my car, got in and started it; flicked the lights on and drove swiftly away, without allowing myself even one glance back towards the pub door.

TWO

I had told Paul I was seeing a Portuguese guy. It was true that he was Portuguese. More specifically, though, he hailed from the Atlantic island of Madeira. His name was Duarte. And, as I had told Paul, we had met only twice.

The first time it was early evening. I had just finished a day in London doing role-plays for an exam at one of the teaching hospitals. I had gone into The Montreal for a pint and, to be honest, on the hunt for sexual opportunity. Nobody had stood out from the crowd as being interesting or desirable when I first looked around the place. All the seats and tables were taken and I was one of a knot of men who stood around the bar, nursing drinks and occasionally looking at, though not talking to, one another. Then, as if from nowhere, someone shouldered his way towards me. He was my size, or a little bit smaller, and had very bright brown eyes, like a robin's. Dark-haired and, I guessed, a few years younger than me, he looked as though he might have been Italian or Spanish. 'Hi,' he said. Then, 'Are you here on your own?'

'Yes,' I said. 'And you?'

'Yes.' He dropped his eyes to the floor for a second, then they looked back up into mine. 'I haven't seen you in here before.'

'I come in from time to time,' I said. I ran an

appraising eye up and down his body. He was wearing a non-descript short coat that was black, rather shapeless baggy trousers that were black too, and he had black shoes that appeared to be a cheap pair of trainers. The interior of the pub was pretty dark, and his appearance actually seemed to intensify the darkness. But he carried a pint glass full of lager in one hand, and that was bright gold and white-frothed, and when he smiled, which he now did suddenly, his teeth were very evident, and very pearly and white.

'Usually on a Tuesday,' he said. It took me a second to realise he was telling me about his own visits to the place.

I half laughed, nervously. 'I'm a bit less regular than that. I live outside London. I usually only call in if I've been up in London working.'

'What work do you do?' he asked, then took a small swallow of beer as he waited for my answer. 'Interesting,' he said, nodding thoughtfully, after I'd told him. I asked him what he did. That's when he told me he was a bus driver. He worked out of Westbourne Park depot, he said. The money was OK but the hours were anti-social.

Without thinking, I corrected him. 'Unsocial.' Then I wanted to kick myself. I really shouldn't do that to people.

He didn't seem to mind, though, or even notice. He said, 'Except Tuesdays.'

It was at that moment that I decided I liked the look of him and liked the way he was talking. Liked those things enough to say, 'I'm Peter.'

'Duarte,' he said. Of course I had to ask him how to spell it. (You might be wondering how to pronounce it. It's Doo-*ar*-tay, with the accent on the middle syllable.) By now we'd shaken hands. But when he'd finished spelling Duarte he unexpectedly touched my shoulder and ran his hand down my upper arm, round the crook of my elbow (my elbow was bent because I was holding my beer glass) and halfway along the outer edge of my jacket-sleeved forearm. Then he withdrew his hand before it encountered the complications of the pint glass among my fingers. 'You're nice,' he said.

I laughed in surprise. And then surprised myself. 'So are you,' I said. The words just popped out: I hadn't planned them.

He raised his right heel off the ground, causing his knee to angle forwards and make brief contact with mine. I said, 'Shall we go downstairs?'

'Why not?' he said, and turned and led the way.

The downstairs bar wasn't usually open this early in the evening. But today... Luck, I suppose. It was even more dimly lit than upstairs, and its walls, ranged around a central dance floor, were lined with cosy sofas. But we went to the bar first. Both our glasses were nearly empty, and Duarte offered to refill them as soon as we arrived. While we stood by the bar waiting for the drinks to be poured I reached into Duarte's crotch and for half a second grabbed what I could. I just wanted to be sure we were on the same page. We were: Duarte snickered and for half a second I felt his hand explore my half-hard dick too.

Sprawling together, cuddling, on a sofa in the half-dark made a pleasant way of passing the next hour. Our hands found their way up under shirts, pinching nipples, and down into trousers, feeling cocks. And everywhere else too. Duarte said, 'I'm sorry if I'm too tactile for you. Some people find me a bit...'

I cut him off. 'You're not too tactile. I like that. I'm the same.' I didn't think anyone could be too tactile for me now. My supplier of hugs and cuddles and kisses had been cruelly removed a year ago. I'd nearly starved.

Talking of starving, we eventually decided we needed something to eat. Reluctantly we re-buttoned our shirts and made our way up the basement stairs and out into the street. Within a couple of blocks we found an Italian restaurant, where we each filled ourselves with a simple pasta dish while sharing a bottle of Veneto wine. 'I'd like to take you back to my place,' I told Duarte. 'But it might not be practical tonight. It's fifty miles away.'

He grimaced. 'And I'm on shift at six in morning. Another time?'

'And you live...?' I prompted him. He'd already told me where – Willesden – but he hadn't told me what.

'It's just a small studio flat. One small fold-down

single bed, and the walls are thin like cardboard. I can't have people there.'

That last bit was disappointing. Willesden was in relatively easy reach. Even if I'd have to tumble out of bed and into the street at five. I'd had no difficulty with sharing single beds before, and both of us were slim. I said, 'Well, when you do get down to mine you'll find I've a whole house to myself. Detached. In the middle of the countryside. You can make as much noise as you like. Scream and shout and no-one'll hear.'

'Sounds scary,' he said.

I looked at him across the table and raised my wineglass. 'Do I look the scary sort?' I asked.

He grinned broadly. 'No, you don't.' I felt him tweak my knee. 'We'll fix a date for me to come down. Maybe in two weeks.' I saw him wriggle then, and he giggled. 'My trousers are all wet inside.'

We didn't wait two weeks. I came up to London the following Sunday and we went for a chilly but friendly walk in Hyde Park. When dusk fell we settled into our pub sofa routine, and had our Italian meal. Then we returned briefly to the pub for one last drink and said our early goodnights (Duarte had another six o'clock start to face in the morning). These 'goodnights' took the same form as they had done the first time we'd met. We went into the pub toilet and wanked each other off side by side at the urinals. We had to keep breaking off when anyone came in, but on both occasions patience was rewarded and we got there in the end. It was better than nothing, but I did look forward – and so did he, he said – to the warmth, comfort and dignity of a shared bed.

I didn't tell many people about Duarte. In a small village you don't need to. I told one of the other staff at the King Billy and, as I already mentioned, I told the guy I met in The Harrow, Paul. While the story would by now be all around the King Billy – which I was fine with – where Paul was concerned it hardly seemed to matter. He lived a couple of villages away, I seemed to remember him saying, and I thought I was unlikely to see him again. It was just a few days after my meeting with him, though, that Duarte came down, halfway to where I lived, by train. 'Get the train to Tonbridge,' I'd told him. 'I'll meet you and drive you the rest of the way from there.'

I met Duarte on the platform and we walked together through the foot-tunnel beneath the road – it seemed extraordinarily long because it was so narrow, and we made the most of it by kissing and embracing all the way – into the car park. I got my keys out and flicked the switch. Lights flashed on a nearby car.

'Oh wow,' said Duarte. 'You drive a Jaguar?'

'It's old,' I said, 'but I love it. I bought it from my best mate. It's beautiful to drive.' I remembered then that my new friend spent his working days driving a double-decker London bus. 'You might find fault with my driving,' I added bashfully.

He gave me a smile I can't describe. 'I doubt it,' he said.

I did show off a bit on the drive home, I must admit. As anyone who has a handsome bus driver as a passenger inevitably does.

We drove straight to the King Billy, where they'd kept the kitchen open specially, and ordered fish and chips. The locals – who were my customers when I worked there – welcomed us with appraising nods and cautious smiles. Duarte wasn't the first pick-up I'd taken there. Mine was a small village. I'd have to be careful about this, I thought.

There wasn't much to be seen of the outside of my house as I drove Duarte up to it. It was March, it was late and it was dark. But the inside pleased him greatly. At least, the size and spaciousness and the décor did. But the temperature gave his Madeiran skin a bit of a culture shock.

I lit the wood-burning stove and, with its doors open, we spent the rest of the evening roasting in front of it. We talked about our plan to get up early, drive to Dover and take the ferry to Calais the following day. I won't go on about the sex we had that night, though I can't resist recording one detail: Duarte, standing naked in the firelight and, facing the open doors of the wood-burner, shooting from his hooded penis a white tracer-arc three feet into the flames. 'It doesn't always go like that,' he said. I didn't care if it didn't. To see that sight once in my life was… I think I have to leave that sentence there.

The drive to Dover wasn't long. But, because of the difference between British and French time, and the time it took to check in in these security-conscious days, and the ninety-minute crossing itself – though its leisurely loveliness was one of the main attractions of this particular day out – we needed to be up at seven and on the road by eight if we were to make it to Calais in time for lunch.

It didn't happen. We stayed in bed till twelve. Because… because we were having a good time where we were. Then we got up and had coffee, and re-planned the day. If we set off for Dover and Calais now, we'd arrive just as it was getting dark. We could have dinner, we reckoned, but it would be midnight before we got back… Duarte's body-clock told him to get up at five and go to bed at nine. We looked at each other and shook our heads. We made a second pot of coffee and went back to bed.

In the evening we braved the knowing looks of the regulars at the King Billy and had another dinner there. There was fresh sea-bass on the menu. Duarte ordered it at once. Madeira is surrounded by sea, but only one fish flourishes in quantity in those deep waters. And it isn't sea-bass.

We'd already exchanged histories by now, Duarte and I. Duarte knew I'd lost my partner of twenty years to lung cancer. 'He didn't smoke,' I heard myself explaining. 'It was just one of those things.'

'Traffic pollution, of course,' said Duarte, casually lighting up a cigarette. My partner hadn't smoked but Duarte did.

Duarte had, like me, enjoyed a long-term relationship with an older man. Duarte had found himself a bit hemmed in eventually – which was something I could at least understand – and had moved out of the comfortable house they'd shared in Highgate in order to do his own thing. *Do his own thing in a rotten little studio with paper-thin walls?* I thought this. I didn't say it. Do his own thing? Have his wank in peace at most, perhaps. I couldn't see it amounting to much more than that.

Duarte still saw his ex quite often. Spent whole days with him in the house in Highgate they'd used to share. Ex-boyfriend, though, was planning to move to Dorset, to retire. Lyme Regis, or somewhere like that.

It crossed my mind that if Duarte was interested in living in a nicer house than his walls-of-paper studio in Willesden he could do worse than move in with me. I wasn't going to say this. That move on my part – even if it should ever come about – still lay several months down the line. But still, I began to think about work opportunities for Duarte in my neighbourhood. Just in case...

There weren't many buses for him to drive. A community bus service existed, staffed by volunteers. Actually, most of the work that was done in my neighbourhood was done by volunteers. There were few real jobs. And the nearest real bus depot was forty miles away.

It wasn't the case, though, that Duarte was merely a bus driver. He was formidably educated. He had a degree in European Literature from the University of Coimbra in northern Portugal. This meant that he'd read sixteen of Shakespeare's plays, where I knew only four. He'd read four of Dostoyevsky's novels. (I'd struggled through Crime and Punishment but that was it.) He'd read Dante's Inferno and Bunyan's Pilgrim's Progress, Don Quixote (in the original Spanish), Robinson Crusoe and Gulliver's Travels. Seven of Charles Dickens's masterpieces, as well as most of Chekov, and Turgenev, and Tolstoy's War and Peace. That's London Transport drivers for you. It's amazing the things you find yourself discussing when you're spending most of your time in bed.

Eventually the time came for me to drive him back to Tonbridge. We did the journey in thirty-five minutes. Had it not been for the traffic and the speed cameras we could have done it in a bit less. But then it might have looked like I was wanting to get rid of him. Which I wasn't. At least, I think I wasn't. I think I got it about right.

THREE

Duarte and I texted each other often during the next few days. We talked about meeting up again at The Montreal, and about his next visit to me. We really would make it to Calais next time, we promised each other. Duarte also suggested I meet up with him and his ex-partner at the house in Highgate. Even that I could stay the night. I found myself wondering at that a bit. Duarte's ex was, he'd told me, a retired police inspector. What would the three of us find to talk about? Or did Duarte have a threesome in mind? I wasn't averse to the idea in principle, but Duarte wasn't a very high-tech person, so had no photos of his ex on his phone, and he wasn't on Linkedin or Facebook. I said I'd await an invitation.

Duarte wrote appreciatively about my nice cosy house in the countryside. He'd been reminded of it when he went back to his ex's place in Highgate. I suggested a meet at The Montreal the next Tuesday. He couldn't make it, he said. And then it all went quiet. I let it go for a few more days. Then texted again. No, he couldn't make the following Tuesday either. Another time, he said. There wouldn't be another time, I knew. I didn't text him back.

I went to The Harrow from time to time. I'd pop in for a pint if I was passing, or if I'd got tired of the company at the King Billy. There was nobody at The Harrow who knew of Duarte's existence, so I didn't have to talk about him to anyone, which was good. Then one evening I went in there and saw someone sitting at the bar alone. Saw his back view only, in jeans and a leather jacket. But I also saw the rather long back of his black-haired head, and knew exactly who he was. To say that my heart leaped would be to overstate things rather, but it did perform a little skip. I hopped up onto the bar stool next to him. 'Paul,' I said.

He turned to me. Flash of coal-black eyes. Then a warm smile. 'Peter.' He put forward his hand, I took it in a businesslike way and shook it for half a second. I looked quickly around, took in the fact that he was on his own again. Just like me. 'Pint of Hophead?' he offered. I liked the fact that he remembered what drink I'd had the last time.

We exchanged a few sentences. Then he asked me, 'How was Calais?'

I laughed. 'We didn't get there,' I said. 'Didn't get up in time.'

He grinned at me. 'I get the picture,' he said. 'Sometimes there's just too much to do before you get out of bed.'

I wondered if he'd had a similar, though heterosexual, experience in the interval since I'd seen him last. I'd bring the conversation round to that in a minute. For now I said, 'It was my first time with a southern

European. A learning curve in some ways.'

'Mmm?' said Paul, sounding interested.

'He had to phone his mother in the morning. Phoning Madeira from inside our bed.'

'While the two of you were...?'

'No, not quite,' I backtracked slightly, while the most extraordinary images flashed across my mind. 'Though we were holding each other quite tightly.'

'I suppose you're lucky he didn't want to go on Skype.'

'I hadn't thought of that,' I said. 'He's not very technologically advanced. Perhaps that's just as well.' Paul chuckled. 'He also turned out to be rather sensitive. To things like the cold, I mean. Kept waking me up in the night and asking for extra blankets. By the time morning came we were pretty much buried alive.'

'And we were talking about that last time,' Paul reminded me. 'Extra blankets in the cold. When you're on your own.' He paused a second and swallowed some beer. 'Which you weren't on that occasion. Is your house extra cold, then?' He gave me a rather narrowed look as he said this.

'No,' I said defensively. 'I have central heating. Though I don't run it through the night usually. It's just a question of where he comes from. Madeira's halfway to the Tropics. His other thing...' I wanted to get Paul away from the idea that I had a cold house. 'His ears are sensitive. I keep an old battery-powered alarm clock near the bed. Don't notice the tick myself. Duarte did. Made me put it in a drawer.'

Paul smiled warmly. 'I wonder if he's quite the right person for you. Are you seeing him again?'

'We were going to,' I said. 'But you know how these things go.' Paul nodded gravely. I told him about the invitation to the ex-boyfriend's house at Highgate, which hadn't materialised. Gave him quite a bit of background there.

'Bet I know what's happened,' Paul said. 'He got a taste for your nice house – cold and noisy though it may be – and remembered what he was missing back in Highgate. Bet he's gone back to his ex.'

I hadn't thought through to that possibility. 'You may be right.' I was genuinely impressed by Paul's insight. But it was time to change the subject. 'What about you? Any adventures to report?'

Paul wrinkled his nose in a self-deprecating way. I hadn't seen him do this before. I found it charming. 'One nice lady. Two nice dinners. Paid for by me. But that was as far as it got.' He brought the conversation back to me and Duarte in a dizzying U-turn. 'I hope your Madeiran friend was impressed by the Jaguar at least.'

'He was,' I said. 'I didn't know you knew I had a Jaguar.'

'You drove off in it after we said goodnight last time,' Paul said. 'Like a scalded cat actually. Or a bat out of hell. One of those. I'd hardly got as far as the door. But I could hardly miss clocking the car.'

'It's lovely,' I said. 'I bought it from a friend.' I didn't want to have to find excuses for the rapidity of my departure that last time. Couldn't tell him I ran away because I wanted to go to bed with him and wasn't able to handle that thought. Didn't want to give him a chance to guess it. I clutched wildly at another thought. 'Yes, Duarte loved the car. And he was fun while he lasted. Nice in bed, too. Though he put his underpants back on when it was time to go to sleep...' Dear God, of all the subjects I could have picked to take Paul's mind off my too-rapid exit from the car-park, why had my mind grabbed at this one?!

Paul's head twisted slightly: a movement suggesting surprise but also a hard-to-conceal interest. 'You sleep in the buff, I suppose?'

My throat made a weird sort of grunt that had to serve as an answer. 'Um... Duarte said he'd be playing with himself all night if he slept like that.'

'And you said?' Paul leaned towards me.

I shrugged. Came clean. 'I told him that was more or less what I did.' Then spontaneously giggled.

I only just heard Paul's own chuckle and his quiet, 'Me too, mate.'

At once we looked each other straight in the eye. It took less than a second for us both to realise we had been far too frank with each other. Too open and self-revealing. A straight bloke and a gay bloke meeting for only the second time, and both times by chance, in a public bar. We knew we would have to draw back a bit. 'How's business?' I asked, with almost unseemly haste. Normally that is not a question that one British guy asks another in a pub. But by contrast with the previous bit of conversation this seemed pretty safe.

Paul jumped at the lifeline I'd offered us both and told me. He'd said he was a builder, he reminded me. Well, he'd been simplifying things. The only building work he was involved with was the maintenance of the various properties he owned. His portfolio included a number of cottages on the Cornish coast which brought him in a fair bit of money from holiday lettings, but which required a good deal of time and effort when it came to upkeep. And then... He told me he owned a residential development on the Spanish coast, near Almería, and another one on the Algarve coast of Portugal...

I cut him off. 'Isn't property in free fall over there these days?' I was worried for him suddenly.

He gave a tight smile that was difficult to read. 'I was one of the lucky ones. All built and occupied before 2008 really kicked in. Yes, there've been a few defaults, but mostly people have sat tight and paid their dues. Mostly British and Germans, which helps.'

I stopped feeling worried for him. This man had to be

seriously rich. I wondered where the money had come from that had enabled him to begin. I drew the line at asking, though. For the moment. Instead, I asked, 'Do you travel down there a lot?'

'A couple of times a year, yes,' he answered coolly, and gave me a searching look.

'Next time, take me with you...' No, I didn't say this. I just found suddenly that I wanted to.

We went on talking after that, until we'd polished off three pints each, and then it seemed the moment had come to leave. Together we walked out into the car park.

'Show me your Jag,' he said suddenly. And I did. Rather proudly opened it up and let him sit in the driver's seat. 'Feels nice,' he said, lightly touching the controls. 'And smells nice too. Leather... You must take me for a spin some day.' He started to get out.

'Be happy to,' I said. I went on, 'What do you drive?' What I meant was, *I've shown you mine, now show me yours*. I was pretty sure that his car wouldn't be something he was ashamed to show me. Not if he owned large chunks of Portugal and Spain.

A moment later we'd reversed roles. I was now sat in the front seat of his Kia Ceed, a car I hadn't heard of before. Equipped with gizmos of all kinds, it also had a wonderful smell – the smell of the brand new. I liked the feel of it, liked the buzz of it, and told him so. 'Give you a ride in this one too, some day,' Paul said as I vacated the cockpit. 'Best in daylight, though. And when we've both had less to drink.'

We were standing together now, in the evening dark and chill, between our two beautiful cars. 'Do this again sometime?' I heard myself say. It came out as a bashful mumble.

'Meet up for a drink, you mean?' Paul checked. 'Yeah. Be nice to.' He paused for a second. Then, sounding vulnerable suddenly, 'Same time next week?'

Something warm raced through my veins as I heard him say that. 'I'd like that,' I said. 'Here?' He nodded, and just to be sure of each other we named the hour and the day. Then we looked at each other. I could feel us both starting towards a farewell handshake, then our bodies considering an embrace but both thinking better of it. So that we ended up simply giving each other a parting nod.

Then we walked away from each other and got into our separate cars. This time I let him start up and leave the car-park first. He turned right when he reached the road; a moment later I arrived at the same place and turned left. I realised then that neither of us had asked where the other lived.

FOUR

'Where's your cute friend?'

'Pardon?' I said, turning to face the voice that had spoken unexpectedly in my ear. It belonged to a tall chap whose hair was scraped back into a ponytail. We were both in the crush at the bar at the Montreal.

The face that the voice belonged to broke into a grin. 'That didn't come out right. I thought both of you were cute. You and the guy you were with last time.'

'Oh, right,' I said. When you're fifty-one and someone lobs the word cute at you, you leap to catch it one-handed and then hang on to it as you would a wind-delivered fifty-pound note. 'My little Madeiran friend.'

'I guessed he was from somewhere down there…'

'Fun while he lasted,' I interrupted, to save time.

'I'm Amos,' the tall stranger said. I didn't know whether that would be his first name or his second. I'd never met an Amos before. He gave me his hand.

I shook it. 'Peter,' I announced myself. I went on, 'There's an Amos in the Bible, isn't there?'

He said, 'There's a Peter too.'

A minute later we were sitting at a table, getting to know each other. Amos was from the Caribbean. He told me that. It was always so dark in the Montreal that otherwise I might not have known. 'I've seen you in here before,' I said. I elaborated slightly. 'I mean I've seen you in the toilet, waving your cock around.' I guessed he was a few years older than me. At our age we had to be bold. Both of us. We'd get nowhere otherwise.

He gave me a rather poignant look. 'And from time to time I've noticed yours.'

I said, 'That's cheered my afternoon.'

We did the next bit. How often did we come here? What were we doing in town? What did we do with the rest of our time? Amos was an interior designer. Lived in Hendon. Another one from the inner suburbs. He was married of course. That's how it was if you came from the Caribbean. One daughter and two sons. Straight in Hendon, gay when he came up to town. I nodded at all of this. It was too familiar for words.

The next bit was better, though. 'I'm working on a place in Knightsbridge. The owner is away. I have the key. Would you fancy ... um ... walking over there?'

'Across the park?' I queried. He nodded. 'Why not?' I said. We were still in late March but it was a fine, if draughty, day. I reached under the table and rubbed my hand encouragingly across his knee. Spontaneously, simultaneously, he did the same to mine.

We didn't hurry our pints, but explored each other's hinterlands a little more. We came round to books. Amos was a fan of Hemingway and Scott Fitzgerald. I sang the praises of E. M. Forster and Virginia Woolf. We were ready to respect each other's tastes but clearly an ocean – the one called the Atlantic – lay between them.

At last we emptied our glasses and set out across the traffic maze of Marble Arch into the park. A kind of Atlantic crossing in itself, the traverse of Hyde Park. A vast expanse of grass, transsected by criss-crossing paths in straight lines, like a pilot's aeronautical chart. Nothing to be seen of the other side at first: it had to be taken on trust. Then one by one appeared the landmarks of the distant shore. The tower block that is Hyde Park Barracks, the Albert Memorial's needle spire, the Hyde Park Corner Hilton, the dome of the Albert Hall.

We talked comfortably as we walked in and out of the late afternoon shadows of the trees, confident of our far horizon, knowing that we were on the road to sex; not needing to touch each other for reassurance, not needing to hasten our steps. How different is age fifty-one from its inverse: age fifteen.

We exited the park via the gate next to the French Embassy, narrowly avoiding being knocked down by a gnat-swarm of cyclists. We crossed the road and headed down into Knightsbridge. Almost opposite Harrods Amos swung us off the pavement into a massive entranceway, pressed a buzzer and we were let in. He nodded in a familiar, confident way to a concierge at a long, polished desk and we took the lift upstairs.

It was the fourth floor, or the fifth, I don't remember

which. Amos unlocked the door with a pristine-looking silver key and, for good measure, a golden coloured one that opened a second lock. We were in a magazine cover of a made-over apartment. Ruched white curtains hung at the windows. Original abstract paintings – the kind I always failed to see the point of – brought brave colour to the pastel walls. Walking on the deep-pile carpets felt like treading through an inch or more of snow. Amos showed me all around. I thought his work here must be nearing its completion: I couldn't see that much remained to be done. The owners must be paying him a fortune, I imagined. They must be – and perhaps Amos also was – extremely rich. Nobody I had ever known well enough to be invited into their home lived in anything like as opulent a style as this. Amos kissed me suddenly on the lips and said, 'Let's make ourselves a cup of tea.'

Amos did that in the kitchen, confidently finding the jar of tea-bags and the tin of sugar in one of the fitted cupboards, and hauling milk out of the gargantuan fridge. We sat together on a sofa in the sitting room and, while bringing our mugs to our lips with one hand each, started to stroke each other's legs with the other. Then Amos reached into a pocket in his jeans and pulled out two tablets wrapped in pharmaceutical plastic and foil. They were pale blue. 'Have one of these,' he said.

'What is it?' I asked, though I knew perfectly well. I'd simply never taken one – or thought I needed one – before.

Amos laughed. 'You know what it is. You may not

need it, and nor may I. But I find it adds a little
something these days. A little staying power.'

'OK,' I said. 'I'm up for staying power.' I accepted
the offer with a mumble of thanks.

'Twenty minutes does the trick,' Amos said. 'Think
we can hold out that long?'

We passed the time with lying cuddling on the sofa,
still fully clothed, and kissing occasionally, still talking
about Scott Fitzgerald and Ernest Hemingway whenever
our mouths were free. And then the thing kicked in. I felt
the gentle shock of it run through me the way I felt a
gear-change in the Jaguar's automatic shift.

We took our clothes off then and padded with our
erections into the master bedroom. Amos told me at this
point that he was sixty, as though it was a matter of
some pride.

'You look very good on it,' I told him, and gave his
very large dick a squeeze to make it clear exactly what I
meant.

We tumbled onto the bed from opposite sides and
different ends. The position in which we found
ourselves, my head between Amos's thighs and his
between mine, made it unnecessary to find words for
what we were going to do.

I've always prided myself on giving a fairly decent
blow-job, even if cocks the size of Amos's do scare me a
little bit. And Amos seemed satisfied by my effort, if the

jubilant way in which he came was anything to go by. But he... Maybe they're well-taught in the Caribbean. At any rate his oral skills, as demonstrated on my own dick that day, were so extremely advanced and so pleasure-giving that I could imagine he had spent a lifetime practising in readiness for this very afternoon.

I came in a hot, delighted flood in the warmth of his mouth, on the back of his tongue. And yet... And yet... When the moment arrived another thought arrived with it, as swift, sudden and unwelcome as a hammer blow to my skull. I wanted this other person, the one whose dark, though grey-streaked, hair I was stroking, the one who held my cock in his mouth, whose cock I held in mine, whose animal warmth I felt along the whole length of myself... I wanted this person not to be Amos. I wanted it to be Paul.

We had exchanged phone numbers when we made that same-time-same-place arrangement for the next week. Either of us could have texted to confirm. Neither of us did. I – and presumably Paul too – being terrified of seeming too eager, too keen. It wasn't as if we were going on a date. So that when I arrived at The Harrow on the day we'd fixed and saw that Paul's car wasn't in the car-park, and nor was he sitting at the bar inside, I had no way of knowing whether he was simply running late or had stood me up. I mean, I did have a way of finding out. I could have texted him there and then. But there was no way I was going to do that. Indeed I could have pressed 'dial number' but there was absolutely no way I was going to do that. I climbed onto a stool and ordered myself a pint of Hophead.

Francis, while he was pulling it, said, 'Your friend not with you tonight, then?'

Dear God, I thought, how finely tuned the engine of pub gossip is. *He's not a friend, exactly,* I could easily have said, but I knew that would have made it worse. *What is he then, exactly?* would have been Francis's next thought. He wouldn't have come out with that to me, of course. He was a good landlord. But he would have raised the question, after I'd gone, with everybody else. That's another part of a landlord's job. So I said, 'Paul? He might be in later, perhaps. Don't really know.' I managed to say this in the tone of voice that said, *Don't really care.*

'Nice lad, Paul,' Francis said. Francis was a few years older than Paul and me, but I was still approvingly conscious of the L-word. I hoped that Francis referred to me as a nice lad when I wasn't around.

'I hardly know him,' I said airily. 'He's in property maintenance or something, isn't he?'

Francis smiled. 'Property maintenance – you could say that. He owns houses all over the continent. On the Costas. Algarve. One of the richest men in Icklesham, though you wouldn't think it to look at him. Or from the way he is.'

So now I knew where Paul lived. Icklesham was a village just two hill-tops away. It was home to some five

hundred souls. It might not be too difficul
the richest men in Icklesham, but even so...
there were no discrepancies between what I
telling me and what Paul already had.

'Yes,' I said, 'he has a modest way with him...' and
realised as the words tumbled out that despite my best
intentions I was letting Francis reel me in. And it also
dawned on me that Paul and I had twice sat at this
counter talking about our love lives, and almost touching
on the subject of our masturbatory habits... A bit of a
chill ran through me. That's the trouble with pubs. You
think you're having an intimate conversation with
someone and that no-one else is taking a blind bit of
notice. But presumably, as the pints go down, so does
your guard, while your voice levels head in the opposite
direction... My negative turn of thought was abruptly
curtailed at that moment. For the door opened and down
the single, awkward, step came Paul, looking everything
I wanted him to look – handsome, modest, and suddenly
smiling a little smile as he caught sight of me.

'I'm a minute late,' he said, the smile turning
mischievous as he came up to the bar and sat on the stool
next to mine. Because of his greater height he didn't
climb onto bar stools the way I did: he just sat on them.

He exchanged nods of greeting with Francis, and I
offered him a pint of whatever he wanted. He'd been
drinking Harvey's the last two times. Now he looked at
my pint searchingly. 'Hophead, is that?' He turned back
to Francis. 'Pint of Hophead, please.' The little things
that tell you the big things. Paul, straight guy that he

as, was growing fond of me.

A minute later, when he'd got his drink and we'd said Cheers together and – more pertinently – Francis had moved away to serve someone else, Paul said brightly, 'I've got an idea. Why don't we just have a couple here and then go into Rye for a meal? As a change from tapas here.' Then his confidence failed suddenly and his tone of voice changed. Became doubtful, subdued. 'I don't know if you'd like that.'

I wanted to hug him. I said, 'I'd like that very much.' Oh dear. Even that sounded a bit eager. A bit gay.

But happily that set the topic of conversation on a convenient path for the next twenty minutes. Restaurants we liked. In Rye. Elsewhere. Favourite cuisines… We decided we'd go to Webbe's Fish Café, assuming we could get in. It wasn't a café at all, we both knew, but a rather up-market fish restaurant that had named itself a café, presumably, in a fit of proletarian chic. I'd been there with my late partner; Paul had been there with his ex.

We talked about parking in the narrow cobbled streets of the small town. Always a nightmare. We agreed we'd play safe and park in the supermarket car-park at the bottom end of town and walk up together. Paul said, 'That gives us two hours before the CCTV clobbers us.'

'That should do,' I said in a businesslike way. I found it difficult to think ahead to the end of those two hours. To how they would end. To how we would part tonight.

We drove in convoy. Always a bonding experience, I've found. And then, when we'd parked – actually in adjacent spaces – we walked together up the hill. A new thing to be striding purposefully along a street with someone you've been on sitting-only terms with up till now.

'So how's your love life been?' Paul asked me almost as soon as we'd set off.

'That'd better wait till we're sitting down,' I said. 'Interesting, but it'll take a while. I turned my head enquiringly towards him as we walked on side by side. 'Yours?'

'Zilch,' he said. Which puzzled me. He was eminently fanciable, I imagined, in the eyes of any woman over about thirty-five and, since he was presumed to be as rich as Croesus, must constitute quite a catch.

We reached the restaurant, went in, and as it was mid-week, managed to sit at a table where we wouldn't be overheard too easily by everybody else. We both looked around us and exchanged a smile of relief. We didn't need to explain the smiles. We were both pleased not to see anyone else we knew.

We ordered a starter of mixed seafood, a sharing platter, then a turbot 'darne' for Paul, and a Spanish hake dish for me. A bottle of Chablis.

As soon as that was open and poured and the wine waiter had left us I embarked on my Amos tale.

'You're kidding,' Paul said, when I described the apartment I'd been taken to. 'It sounds like a fairy tale.'

'It might do if he'd been a lad of thirty,' I said. 'But, bless him, he was nearly ten years older than me. Nice enough, and gave a great blow-job, but at our age we take what we can get.'

Paul looked across at me. Gave me one of the most searching looks I'd had from him yet. It was hard to interpret it, and I thought perhaps I'd better not try. At any rate, I did notice, there was no smile involved.

I told him the whole story, including the sixty-nine episode. I only left out the Viagra bit, for reasons of personal vanity, and of course I didn't tell him that at the moment of climax I found myself thinking of – found myself wanting – him.

Paul took a large swallow of Chablis, then asked, 'And how did you... I mean, how did you say goodbye?'

That struck me. In all sorts of ways. Paul genuinely wanted to know how the episode had ended. And he was evidently thinking, just as I was, of how he and I were going to say goodbye tonight. He might not have known that he was thinking that. But I knew he was.

I told him. 'He got a towel from the bathroom. Fleecy and fresh. And we mopped up. We could have showered together but ... you know ... the time for intimacy was past. You sort of know when you're saying, till next time, and when it's goodbye.'

Paul nodded his head vigorously. He knew exactly. He was forty-eight. Of course he knew.

But then he looked earnestly into my eyes. He didn't know. Not about us, he didn't. He was forty-eight, but about *us* he didn't have a clue. I was fifty-one. And neither did I.

The food was excellent. We even had a pudding. I know that I enjoyed it but, the funny thing is, I never seem to remember what the pudding was. Paul made a point of calling for the bill before I had thought of it. He got his wallet out and thwacked it on the table in the macho sort of way that some people do with their cocks. And he said, in a tone that indicated that he meant it, 'It's on me.' He permitted himself a smile. It turned surprisingly intimate. 'Next time, you, if you want to do it again.'

There was nothing I could have wanted more. I said, 'Next time, me.'

We walked down the road together. The evening air had chilled startlingly. We didn't say much as we walked. When we did our words escaped as steam.

We got to our cars. We heard the lonely clunk of doors unlocking in response to our keys' commands. Then Paul said it. I wouldn't have dared. He did. 'D'you want to come back to my place for one?'

He meant a drink. I knew he meant that. I didn't allow even my eyebrows, let alone my eyes, to suggest that I perceived a ho-ho double-entendre. 'Yeah,' I said.

'Though I don't know where you live.' OK, I had been told. But not by Paul.

'Icklesham,' said Paul.

'That's fine,' I said. 'Just two hills away. I'll follow you.' And I did.

FIVE

Paul's house was what I, who lived in a Victorian cottage, would have called 'modern'; meaning that it had been built in my lifetime: probably in the nineteen-seventies or eighties, I guessed. I didn't see much of the outside of it, as it was dark, and I couldn't get much of an idea as to what it had in the way of a garden. But the interior was spacious, lit up brightly when Paul racked the dimmer-switches up, and welcoming. It was chilly, though, when we first entered, but Paul pressed a button on the wall the moment we got into the hall and said, 'It'll warm up now in no time.' Which it did.

Paul's living room was furnished tastefully. It didn't scream wealth at you, although it clearly hadn't been got together by a student or a pauper. It was nothing at all like the opulently decorated apartment I'd been taken to by Amos, and I was rather relieved by that.

'What'll you have for a nightcap?' Paul asked, at the same time motioning to me to sit down on one of the three sofas.

'Tell me what you've got,' I said, sitting down and sinking rather deep. *What'll you have* is an awkward question to have to answer if you're in someone's house rather than in a bar or pub.

'Gin and tonic, whisky, canned lager, wine – red or white… Er, that's about it.'

'Sounds enough to be going on with,' I said. 'What about a glass of red? Unless you want something else and you'd have to open the bottle just for me.'

'Glass of red'll do me fine too.' Paul disappeared into a kitchen I had only glanced inside on the way in. Half a minute later there was a popping sound and then he returned with an opened bottle of claret and two gleaming glasses that were fashionably over-big. He sat down on the sofa opposite me, putting the glasses on the coffee table between us, and filled them unfashionable full. 'St-Emilion,' he said. 'Hope that's OK.' Of course it was. By now I'd probably have shared a bottle of paint-stripper with him.

We talked about cars. (Gay men aren't supposed to be able to do this, but I can get by, just about. I have other friends who are straight.) We talked about the housing market, and the trials and tribulations of property developers in the Iberian Peninsula. Paul on his home turf. I told Paul a little more about the work I did in training medics. 'So much is down to communication,' I told him earnestly, and he nodded earnestly back. He poured us a second large glass of wine.

We didn't talk about football and I was glad of that. It's a subject on which I had almost nothing to say, as I knew very little and cared even less. I didn't know whether the same went for Paul, or whether he was conscious of the fact that most gay men don't follow the game and was being sensitive... I was grateful either way. Instead we got onto gardening and the ever-changing nature of the English language. Paul held up the bottle of St-Emilion and looked through it at the light. 'No point leaving that,' he said, and poured the remaining couple of inches into our two glasses, squatting down on his haunches to make sure he was dividing it equally.

There was something wonderful for me about this evening. Especially this moment of it. Since Graham's death only the company of my neighbour and friend Finbar had made me feel warm and comfortable. There had been limits to that: Finbar was a hundred percent straight. That hadn't stopped me from falling for him a little bit. I loved his company ... and now I was finding that, almost as much as Finbar's company, I was enjoying Paul's...

And so we killed the bottle, and it became time for me to go. I said so, and got up, and Paul made no attempt to make me stay, but got up also and walked with me into the hall. I turned to him there. 'Next week, why not come and have a meal with me? I'm a good cook.' It was the wine talking, making me bold. I managed not to add, *No-one to cook for these days.* Fortunately the wine hadn't pushed me as far as that.

He didn't say yes, he didn't rummage for excuses, he asked, 'Where do you live?'

'Two miles past The Harrow. Stay on the Battle road.' I gave him details of how to spot the house and where to park.

'Yep,' he said briskly. 'That'll be nice. I don't eat

cabbage or baked beans.'

I said, 'I won't be doing those.' We walked out together onto his gravel drive. His outside lights came on automatically. It was surprisingly mild: after red wine the weather often turns that way. 'Text me if you can't make it,' I said. I pointed and pressed my car key, and the Jaguar winked reassuringly at me as the locks clicked back. Paul was standing very close to me. I turned towards him. 'Thanks for a great evening,' I said. 'I had a great time.'

'Me too,' said Paul. 'Look forward to next week.'

'Meet at The Harrow first?' I said. 'Seven o'clock?'

'Um…' He hesitated. Then, 'Be awkward for you if you're cooking, won't it? Why don't I come straight to yours? I'll bring a bottle and a can or two.'

He doesn't want people to see us leaving the pub together a second time, I thought. Because of what they'll say about us. Because of what they'll think. I said, 'My place it is, then. Seven o'clock.' There was a silence then and neither of us moved. Suddenly I said, 'Give me a hug.' My voice told both of us that I was on the edge of tears.

I felt Paul's long arms wrap themselves around me at once. So immediate was his move that it seemed he'd just been waiting for my command. I almost thought that if I hadn't said it, that if the still silence had gone on another ten seconds he might have hugged me anyway.

And so we found ourselves standing together in a tight clinch that neither of us seemed to want to break. For how long? Ten seconds? Twenty or more? (Has anybody ever tried counting the seconds?) But at last we did break it. Or, if I'm strictly honest, Paul did. But gently. We stood looking at each other a second longer. Paul had a rather astonished look on his face. I probably had something similar on mine.

'Till next week, then,' I said.

'Drive safely.'

'Take care.'

'Goodnight.'

'Sleep well.'

'Stay warm.'

'Cheers.'

I was in the car by now and closing the door. I drove home like a seventeen-year-old. It took no time at all.

I wouldn't have served him baked beans in any case, though I might have done a dish involving cabbage. I have a lovely Italian recipe in which minced beef and pork are wrapped in parcels of blanched Savoy cabbage leaves, secured with a cocktail stick and gently cooked in butter. I was grateful for Paul's heads-up.

I decided on a starter of smoked salmon and cottage cheese, followed by something that is dead simple but looks a treat: pan-fried duck breasts, sliced onto a bed of Puy lentils that have been bubbled up with onions, sage leaves, lemon juice and white wine. You can do this one-handed while holding a gin and tonic in the other hand and chatting to guests at the same time. Green salad on the side. Warm baguette to mop the juices. Blackberry crumble (it's the only pudding I know about) to follow if we both still had room...

I weakened. I did text him. On the morning of the day. *Still on for this evening?* He texted back. *Sure. See yu 7.* I drove to the supermarket then, to get the stuff. I felt the car floating about a foot above the road.

The doorbell rang, not at seven but at ninety seconds past. His timing was wonderful. I let him in.

Everybody drinks gin and tonic. I didn't give him a choice in the matter, just handed the glass to him. 'It's nice,' he said, folding his long legs around a chair. He didn't mean the gin and tonic: he was looking appreciatively round the room.

'It was nicer when there were two of us here,' I said, only realising how crass that was after I'd said the words. I wasn't the only one who'd recently found himself living alone.

'Don't I know,' he said. He was smiling, but the reproach was there.

I opened the doors of the wood-burning stove. Having

the doors open runs away with the log pile but it improves the atmosphere no end. I had to will away the memory of Duarte shooting his load into the flames. 'I'm doing baked beans in a cabbage-leaf wrap,' I said, poker-faced.

He looked at me gravely. He said, 'I might even eat it if you did.' My God, that gave me a jolt.

I had to introduce my boyfriend of course. Dead he might be but there were pictures of him, captured at various points in his life, on the walls. 'He was handsome,' was Paul's eventual verdict, delivered after a thoughtful pause. 'Lucky you.'

There was no answer to that. I didn't attempt one. 'We're eating in the dining-room,' I said. 'Hope that isn't too formal for you.'

'Puts the gilt on the gingerbread,' he said. I'd never heard the expression used like that before. Takes the gilt *off* the gingerbread, yes... Somehow I guessed it was something Paul had never said before.

Nobody ever complains if you give them smoked salmon, unless they take a moral stance on eating fish, and Paul was as happy with his starter as I was. As well as the white Macon-Villages we drank with it.

We drank a bottle of burgundy with the duck. Paul had brought it with him. It was a Grands Echézeaux 2011. Paul said that it was exceptional value among the burgundies. The difficulty people had pronouncing it kept the price down.

I'd never heard of it. I didn't attempt to pronounce it. Neither did Paul. We just read the label together. And it tasted more than fine.

Somehow we made room for the blackberry crumble. It completely changed the taste of the Echézeax, but neither of us was going to complain. And then we returned to the living-room. I put some music on. I didn't give Paul a chance to talk about his musical tastes, which might, for all I knew, have been upsettingly different from mine. I put on Mozart. Nobody dislikes Mozart. Same as gin and tonic. I had a CD of some of the piano concertos. Nobody ever walks out of the room when you play those.

'Been back to that pub of yours in London?' Paul asked. 'The one where you pick up men from all around the world?'

'No,' I said. Then I stopped. 'Actually,' I admitted, 'I almost did. Had a day's work in London on Saturday. Took the tube to Marble Arch, meaning to go to The Montreal. I got as far as the door, but couldn't face going in there. Turned round. Tubed back to Charing Cross and came home.' I eyeballed Paul, sitting in the opposite armchair, challenging him to make of that story what he would. I could see him taking it in. I knew the cogs were whirring in his brain. I was only now beginning to understand why I'd balked at entering The Montreal. I wondered if perhaps he too was getting there.

'You'll have to take me The Montreal one day,' he

said. Of all the things he might have said that was probably what I'd have expected least.

I said, 'I've got some Jack Daniels, or Madeira, or another bottle of red.'

'Better not mix it,' he said, sounding rather serious. 'You OK to open another bottle of red?'

I was more than OK with that. 'Rioja all right?' I asked.

'Live on it over there,' said Paul.

While I was out in the kitchen uncorking it Portia appeared. Clicked through the cat-flap and streaked into the living room. I heard Paul's voice say, 'Hey, who's this then? You didn't tell me you had a...' And then Portia streaked right past me again, aghast at the unexpected presence in the living-room, and twanged back out through the cat-flap.

I apologised on her behalf. 'She's funny with strangers,' I called through the open door. 'Especially strange men.'

I re-entered the living room with the bottle just as Paul was saying, 'Well, yes. I guess I'm one of those.'

Even if I'd had three sofas, like Paul had, we wouldn't have been sitting on the same one. So why did I find myself getting fretful about the fact that we were sitting in separate armchairs? Because I found I wanted to be close to him. Even on the bar stools in The Harrow we sat close enough to touch, but here, in the privacy of my home, we could not do that. Unless I were to pick up the chair I sat in and move it closer to his... My mind boggled at the thought. Nobody, ever, anywhere, does that. I'd never read of it happening in a book, or seen it in a film. 'What's making you smile?' Paul asked.

'Nothing,' I said. I couldn't possibly tell him. I refilled his glass instead while, on the CD that was playing, Alfred Brendel launched into the glorious sunshine of K488 in A. It has three movements. All are wonderful. We didn't need to talk. We basked in Mozart like sunbathers on a beach. All that was necessary was for me a couple of times – and Paul once – to top our glasses up.

The CD ended. So did the bottle. We looked across at each other. I thought Paul's face was rather expressionless. 'I'd better go,' he said. His voice was expressionless too.

'I've got a spare room,' I said matter-of-factly. 'If you don't want to drive.' The words came out so smoothly, I might have been practising them for years. Perhaps I had.

'No, I'd better go,' he repeated, but he didn't get up. We sat and looked across at each other, stony-faced, for maybe a minute. One of us would have to make a move. I discovered, as I found myself getting to my feet, that it was going to be me.

I stood in front of him while he continued to sit,

slumped a little, in his chair. 'Better get you standing up, then,' I said. I took his arms and he stood up with me. He didn't need my help to stand up, but neither did he shake loose from my clasp. And when we were standing up, facing each other, we hugged.

A long while we stood like that, folded in each other's arms. Did he then, consciously or otherwise, angle his cheek down and towards me? I fingered it with awe. And then I kissed it. He didn't respond. He didn't react. He didn't pull away. He said, 'You know, I'm not sure if I ought to be driving home.'

I was making a supreme effort to play it cool. 'You don't have to. Like I said.'

SIX

At that moment he leaned down and kissed me.

Not on the cheek, as I'd kissed him, but on the lips. He made no attempt to get his tongue inside them, and I certainly wasn't going to force things at my end. It was the kind of kiss we might have exchanged with our mothers while saying goodnight when we were children.

My right hand was less circumspect than my tongue. Seemingly unbidden, it reached into the crotch of Paul's jeans and found Paul's cock. It wasn't hard, but it wasn't entirely soft either. It dangled, and was long.

I felt Paul's fingers explore, then close around, mine. He said, close in my ear, 'How many rooms have you got upstairs?'

I was going to giggle or I was going to cry. I giggled. But it was close. I said, 'How many do you think we'll need?'

'Maybe one'll do.' He didn't so much speak the words as nuzzle me with them.

I was three inches less in height than Paul but I was three years older. I took charge. I said, 'Follow me.'

We stood in my bedroom, facing each other. Very methodically, as though we did this together every day, we removed pullovers and the shirts that hid beneath. Neither of us had a vest or T-shirt on under that, so we now stood bare-chested and bare-armed, facing each other. Scrutinising each other rather carefully. Because Paul was approaching fifty and I had just passed it, the likelihood was that we'd each find the other carried a substantial paunch. Rather wonderfully – and we could almost hear each other's sigh of surprise and approval – neither of us did. Well ... er ... actually we did have paunches. But only very small ones. (Even if bigger than your average twenty-year-old's.) But because they were very small, and because they were of equal size (or smallness) we were prepared generously to overlook them. It was as if, in being the same size, they cancelled each other out.

Had I been twenty years younger I'd have taken my socks off next. That would have been because, with my slender legs, I looked better trouserless and sockless than with trousers off and socks still on. These days, though, I no longer cared. And also, these days, I found it easier to take my socks off sitting down. It was clearly the same with Paul. Simultaneously we unfastened our own jeans and pulled them down. Then looked across at each other, surveying the damage the years had done. We both had the same thought: I felt it in the room. The thought was: *Could have been much worse.*

There was a bit of a surprise though, for both of us. I mean, I knew I wasn't wearing underpants. I would never have guessed, though, that neither was Paul. And the same, obviously, went for him.

His cock was beautiful. By now it was quite straight and, though only at seven o'clock, was showing promise of things to come. I reached forward and took it in my hand, in a civilised sort of way, like someone shaking hands. Paul did the same with mine.

'Let's get you horizontal,' said Paul. It was a good idea, for many reasons. One of those was that, because we'd had so much to drink, it was no longer very easy for us to stand.

We more or less fell onto the bed. I had no intention of trying to fuck my unexpected new bed-mate. Even if I was physically able to by this time, there was the question of his straight-cred and dignity. He was going to feel bad about this in the morning anyway. If he had to look back on a passive fuck as well... That might have been too much of a night to remember.

On the other hand he might try and fuck me. That's what straight men usually did when they went to bed with someone, of whatever sex. For the moment we were simply rolling and cuddling on the top of the bed. I tried to gauge from the feel of his body and his movements what he actually wanted to do. The impression I got was that what he wanted to do most was to fall asleep.

But no. I felt his hand on my hard cock at that moment, and instinctively I put mine around his. We started to masturbate each other, making contented little 'mmm' noises in between the kisses we were dabbing on each other's lips...

The next thing I knew, it was the small hours and Paul

was asleep and purring calmly next to me. One of us had evidently managed to get us under the duvet. Paul probably. But he hadn't put out the bedside light. I did that now. Then I wrapped myself around the warm sleeper at my side. This was almost certainly the last time I'd find myself in this situation with Paul. I was determined to get from it what I could. The nice thing – the lovely thing – was that as soon as I got my arms around Paul he put his round me, and put one leg over mine, which was much more than I'd expected. More than, until a few hours ago, I'd have even dreamed of. Experimentally I reached in between us for his cock, but that was an optimistic step too far. There would be nothing happening there. It still felt nice, though.

I awoke in a momentary confusion about where I was and what was happening to me. I was literally being shaken awake. Outside it was getting light. I was lying on my side, Paul spooning me from behind, his morning-stiff cock thrusting in and out between my thighs, while his arm was reaching around and masturbating my morning hard-on at the same time.

Neither of us spoke. I felt Paul's body kick down a gear as he approached his climax, and then felt his sudden wetness between my legs and at the back of my balls. That triggered my own orgasm, and I pumped out into the duvet cover and over the sheet. Then Paul relaxed, though he stayed where he was. Still neither of us spoke. We both went back to sleep.

'Have to be up and going.' Paul's voice woke me up. He was standing beside the bed, hauling himself quickly into his clothes.

I blinked at the bedside clock. 'It's only seven,' I said. 'Have a coffee before you go, at least.' I sat up, brought my legs round and put my feet on the floor. I felt a little reminder-shock of his wetness near my arse.

Paul pushed me gently back into the bed. He bent down and kissed me, and all but tucked me up. 'Go back to sleep, Peter. Get some rest.' He was smiling. There was something of wonder in his eyes, something of delight. 'I have to go, though. Your driveway's very open to the road. My car can't be seen here. I'll get some coffee when I'm home. I'll let myself out.'

Of course I didn't allow him to do that. I scrambled naked down the stairs behind him, opened the front door, though I prudently half hid behind it, and kissed him one last time on the cheek, before closing the door after him. Then – it'll be when he gets home to his empty house and makes his coffee that he'll start to hate himself, I thought. Glumly I made some coffee in my own empty house and took it back to bed with me.

I didn't shower for three days.

I did talk to Hannah, though. Hannah worked with me at the King Billy. She heard about the trials and tribulations of my love life and I head about hers. I told her about the not-showering thing. 'It's not an extreme I'd go to myself,' she said, 'but I can understand the sentiment behind it. Do you think it'll...? I mean, do you think anything more will...?'

'I sent him a text later that morning, but no reply.'

'Give him time,' Hannah said. She was twenty years younger than me, but sometimes twenty years cleverer.

I gave him five days. Then I texted again. *Want to meet at the Harrow?* Usual day, usual time. He texted back. *If you don't mind I'd rather not.*

To this day I don't know if it would have hurt more to hear nothing than to hear that. But I wasn't a quitter. Gamely I drove to The Harrow on the usual evening. I would give him the option of changing his mind and, if he did questingly approach The Harrow, of finding me there.

I ordered my pint of Hophead. 'Paul joining you?' asked Francis as he pulled it.

'Don't know,' I said. 'Maybe.' There are moments when you feel very exposed.

I sat drinking my beer, deep inside myself for most of the time, though occasionally exchanging a sentence with Francis or another customer with whom I was on sentence-exchanging terms. I had a second pint, and some tapas to mop it up with. I realised that "he wasn't coming" must be a cliché as old as Adam and Eve. But the reality is different. You never ever admit to yourself that the other person isn't coming. You just accept that the moment has arrived when you must go home. And eventually that is what I did.

I had a task for the following morning, and determined to do it as soon as I got up. It involved Portia. Before he died Graham had made the back garden as nearly escape-proof as was possible, cat-wise, given that cats are Houdini-like, and that Portia was a cat. But in the last few days Portia had managed to find a way, by means of a rotted board behind the garage, out of the garden and into the road, on the other side of which the grass was very green and the rabbits well-fed, and along which the cars ran very fast.

Portia arrived on my bed during that night, around four a.m. I wasn't unhappy to be woken up by her. I reached out and put my arm around her. I was lucky to have her, I thought. I went back to sleep.

I woke up again to hear two people talking in the road. I couldn't hear what they were saying but I recognised their voices. One belonged to a woman who lived a few doors away on the other side; the other to my friend Finbar, already mentioned, who lived three doors away on my side. Finbar and I had become such good friends since Graham died that I now thought of him as my closest friend in the world. As well as falling in love with him a little bit... It was he who had sold me his old Jaguar. I was a little surprised to hear him talking in the road with the woman from opposite. I didn't know they even knew each other...

The knock at the door came very loud. I stumbled out of bed and opened the window. Naked, I leant out of it. The morning air felt very cold. Below me stood Finbar at my front door. He looked up. He wasn't smiling. Grimly he said, 'You'd better come down.'

Jeans pulled on, a coat and wellingtons...

'Bad news,' Finbar said when I met him on the doorstep. 'I think it's Portia.'

I grabbed hold of Finbar, though it wasn't something I'd ever done with him before. He all but shook me off. 'Come on,' he said. 'We need to check.'

We crossed the road together. There was Portia, lying on her side, partially disembowelled. As I picked her up her guts, those private parts of her that I was never supposed to see, came spilling out of her like an endlessly unravelling ball of twine. Together we carried her back across the road. Finbar found a bin bag and we put her in it. 'We'll leave her here for now,' I said.

Finbar surprised me by putting his arms round me. 'Do you want to come in for a coffee?'

Ten days ago I'd have taken him up on that most eagerly. I'd have sat with him on his sofa and demanded to be cuddled while I cried my heart out. But the week that had intervened had turned everything on its head. I heard myself saying, 'If you don't mind, there's someone else I want to see.' And yes, I felt like a louse.

Finbar looked at me carefully. 'Are you sure you'll be OK? Because if you're not...'

'Thank you,' I said. 'If I get no joy where I'm going...'

'Call on me,' said Finbar. 'You seem a bit... Well, if there's anything you need...'

'Thank you,' I said. Untypically, ungratefully, I just wanted him to go.

I drove at breakneck speed to where Paul lived. Just four miles away as the crow flew, it was more than double that by narrow twisting roads, and a river bridge lay in between... I had no reason to suppose he'd be home at eight in the morning. I didn't know his habits well. I drove in through his open gate and, spinning pebbles up under my wheels, came to a stop on his gravel drive. His car was there. I barely took it in. There was a bell beside his door. I didn't bother with it. My fists rained hammer blows upon his door.

A moment later he stood in front of me. His face fell apart when he saw me. He looked like someone crushed between two millstones. 'You,' he said, without expression. 'What are you doing here?'

'I've lost Portia,' I said.

'Who's Portia?' he asked impatiently.

'My cat,' I said. 'You met her. But she wasn't my cat.

She was Graham's.'

'Graham?'

'My fucking boyfriend. The one who died.' I might have burst into tears then. But I didn't. Instead I howled. A howl of animal pain rose up from a place inside me that I hardly knew was there. It had happened to me a few times in the days before and after Graham died. Each time I'd managed to shut it back down. But now it was happening in a public – yet still intensely private – way. It was happening between me and Paul. And this time I couldn't stop it. A year of grief was welling up inside me and bursting out. I didn't know when this would end, or if it would, or how it could.

Paul stood in front of me, frozen with shock, staring into my face with wide, startled eyes. Then he moved forwards and took me firmly in his arms. He said, 'You'd better come inside.'

SEVEN

We sat together on one of his sofas. Paul's arm was around my shoulder, my head was on his chest. In the deep silence I could hear and feel the quiet beating of his heart.

I wasn't quite sure how we'd ended up here. I'd gone into the house with Paul, had stood beside him in the kitchen while he made us both coffee. We'd hardly spoken. The words, 'Fucking shit,' had made their way out of me amongst my occasional sobs. Paul had asked me if I wanted sugar and milk. I'd kept my arms firmly stuck to my sides to stop myself from throwing them around him again, which was what I wanted to do. Then he had carried both mugs of coffee into his living-room, indicated with his head where I should sit, and then, after putting the mugs on the low table in front of us, placed himself next to me and silently drawn me into him with one encircling arm.

And so we sat for a long time, neglecting our coffee till it had gone cold, in a silence so intense that we could hear the garden birds chirruping outside, along with the steady throb of Paul's heart and the singing, like a distant kettle, of the blood in my own veins. At last Paul broke the spell. 'I'm sorry,' he said.

I didn't reply to that, and so a further minute of silence ensued. This time it was a tenser silence, as if someone had tightened a wire. Then Paul spoke again.

'Let's go upstairs.'

He led me straight into his large-bedded bedroom, so there was no doubt about what – roughly speaking at any rate – we were going to do. We stripped off in a businesslike way, watching each other carefully, beadily trying to gain access to each other's thoughts, though without success on either side. We were not evenly matched on this occasion, though. My penis remained soft while Paul's was flamboyantly hard. He came towards me and lifted me easily off the floor. He was considerably bigger than me and, presumably stronger. I was light, even for my size, and had always been easy to carry. Even Graham, who was not much bigger than me, had found me eminently portable.

I wrapped my legs around Paul's waist, expecting him to throw me onto the bed. But he did not. To my surprise he hoisted me higher – with a bit of an effort I have to say – and sat me on the top of his chest of drawers. Then he raised my legs until I rolled backwards a bit, he expertly found my anus with a spit-moistened finger and, when he'd worked his way around inside it and judged me to be sufficiently relaxed, removed the finger and replaced it with his cock, which seemed at this moment very alarmingly long.

It went in very easily, I was glad to discover, and the chest of drawers seemed to be at a very comfortable height, and he seemed to find this a very natural way to be doing things, was very confident of the choreography. I guessed he'd done the same thing – or something similar – in the same place, with his ex-girlfriend.

Still neither of us spoke. Paul pumped me thoughtfully and quite slowly, only speeding up just before the end. During those few minutes we continued to gaze, although without smiling, into each other's eyes. After he had shot his load inside me Paul reached forward and ruffled my hair and fingered my nose. Then he said, diffidently, 'Shall we get into bed?' I nodded my silent yes, and then he pulled himself out of me and helped me down onto the floor. We slipped naked in between the covers. It was not until we had drawn together and were embracing tightly that I found my cock was hard...

After what happened next we spent the rest of the morning just lying together. From time to time Paul's phone, which seemed to be in his jeans pocket on the floor, would fart to acknowledge the arrival of a text, or play a jolly tune on receipt of a phone call, but Paul took no notice of any of them. My own phone was probably doing the same. I had no way of knowing. In my rush to drive to Paul I'd simply left it at home.

Our silent fucking, our silent cuddling, kissing and stroking of each other, was the balm that began – though only began – to heal the hurt that Portia's death had done me. It could only be a beginning, though. Portia's death was the echo of Graham's death a year ago, and it would take more than a morning in bed with someone, even someone as lovely as Paul, to mend the wound of that.

We dozed off intermittently in each other's arms and might have gone on doing this all day, but around noon I sensed a purposeful tautening of the limbs that Paul was wrapping round me, and understood from this that he was about to make some sort of move. Like get out of bed, or speak. He spoke first. 'Perhaps we should do something constructive now,' he said. 'Like have a gin and tonic.' Then he got out of bed.

We were back on the sofa downstairs again. We'd pulled on jeans and a sweater each, but nothing else: no underpants, no socks, no shoes. We were sipping from large glasses, which contained more gin than tonic actually, though mercifully diluted by enough ice to sink the Titanic – ice which clanked and tinkled as we raised the glasses to our lips. Paul said, 'You've been in a bad place this morning. I know you still are. It wasn't just about Portia. I know that. It was Graham.' He stopped, then said in a smaller, more fragile, voice, 'I've been in a bad place too.'

'I know,' I said. I laid my arm across his shoulder and stroked the nape of his neck. There's a little bump at the base of each side of the skull that you never notice when you look at people. You only think about it when you stroke their necks. On some people it doesn't feel so good. On others it is beautiful. The bump I felt at the base of Paul's skull was one of the beautiful ones. I said, 'I know where you are.'

He didn't acknowledge that. 'Perhaps I could be gay. Perhaps I should be gay. Camp it up a bit. Go round swinging a handbag…'

I cut him off a bit irritably. 'Do I do that? Do you know many gay men who do that?'

'Sorry,' he said. 'And no, of course. The answer to both your questions is no. But I can't... I mean, living here in the countryside, a business to run, I can't have people in pubs telling each other as soon as I walk out of the door that I'm the straight guy who has a boyfriend.'

I didn't know how to reply. He had put a week of thoughts and private doubts and agonies into one sentence. It couldn't be answered in a sentence. It would require another week. I said, 'Would you come on holiday with me?'

That threw him onto the back foot in his turn. He said, 'What do you mean?'

He'd used the word boyfriend. That had set my own head spinning. Was that what he had been thinking about himself and me? That we were – even if he thought we shouldn't be – boyfriends? My heart leapt, flattered by the very idea of that. Yet was it any less outrageous than what I'd been thinking on the same front? Wishful thinking. Subconscious thinking. Trying-not-to-think-it thinking.

I tried not to think now. Tried to let the words come out unguarded. 'I mean spend a week away together. Somewhere nobody knows us. Where people won't talk behind their hands when we're in a bar together.' I had to bring my lips under control before I could say the next bit. 'I don't have – any more – a cat to worry about, to put in a cattery. I could put work off for a bit. You could... I mean we could go to one of the places where you've got property, Almería or the Algarve. I'm sure you've got work you could do down there. It'd be a business trip. Claim expenses…'

He said decisively, 'Fuck all that. We'll go to Italy. I've never been there. Always wanted to go…' Then he faltered. 'I'm sorry. I was talking for myself. Not thinking about you. You might not want to go to Italy at all.'

I said, 'I've been to Italy. But I'd love to go again. I'd love to go there with you.' And I heard myself sounding soft and subdued: sounding like someone who might actually camp it up a bit in the streets of Milan or Bologna, and swing a handbag. And then I leaned into his shoulder, buried my face in his neck and soaked his sweater with a deluge of tears.

For the rest of that day we talked. We drove together to my house, talking. This was the grim bit. In the garden Portia awaited us, wrapped in a bin-liner. We shared the digging, in a spot she had liked to sit in, under an old pear tree. We covered her grave with fire bricks to stop foxes digging there. Then Paul kissed me and we drove back to his. We toasted cheese under the grill and talked. We drank a glass of wine in the garden during a brief sunny interval and talked some more. We went for a walk… We took a path that led through apple orchards towards a high spot where there was a windmill. From there we looked out across the English Channel, sparkling silver, and before it a long chain of landmarks on the English coast. Dover's white cliffs. Dungeness point. Rye Harbour, where the river Rother struggles against the shingle into the sea. The wetland lakes on Pett Level. Fairlight cliff, forbiddingly dark...

Don't say it, I thought. It's far too soon for that. Instead, I gave him my email address and the number of my landline. In this topsy-turvy world, in which everyone has your mobile phone number at their immediate disposal, these are intimate things to do. Paul then made those same intimate advances towards me.

For our evening meal we drove a little distance – ten miles or so – to a pub in a village where nobody knew either of us. It seemed a wise thing to do. It was certainly a good choice when it came to the dinner. We had a beautifully rare steak each, and a raspberry frangipane tart, with a deliciously unhealthy quantity of cream. But we hadn't been quite prudent enough when it came to choosing the venue. We hadn't travelled far enough. Hannah, who I worked with at the King Billy, came in with her boyfriend. The space was too small and cosy for us to ignore each other. Paul had to be introduced. As 'a friend'. I didn't say more than that. But it was significant enough in village gossip terms. At least there was a limit to the damage done. Neither of the others knew Paul. But he could easily be described, and was noticeably slim and tall.

After our meal we drove back, making a detour to pass my own house so I could grab a toothbrush and a change of clothes, to spend the night at Paul's. And, despite the knowledge that I'd have to get up early and remove my car from Paul's driveway at first light, we spent a very good night indeed.

There were two issues to be dealt with, it seemed, before I could consider myself as being in a relationship with Paul. (A fling is no problem; you can have a fling with anyone; but by now I wanted more.) There was the problem of Paul's not being able to be seen with me, or not wanting to be seen with me, and the question of whether Paul was gay enough to have a relationship with me at all. The two things were as closely connected as a horse and a cart, but which was which was, for now, impossible for me to say. I spent the next few days ruminating on these difficulties and so, of course, did Paul.

I tried to imagine myself in Paul's position. It wasn't at all hard to do. He had broken up with a female partner after twenty years. He was on a dating website, trying to meet the right woman to spend the next part of his life with. Perhaps the whole of the rest of it. The last thing he needed, when that was his objective, was to get sidetracked by a dalliance with a man. Being seen around the place with me, an openly gay guy, would fatally puncture his credibility as a potential partner for those women of the neighbourhood or on the internet who might otherwise regard him as a good catch. (I regarded him as a good catch. Just in case that isn't apparent yet...) I could also see that it might damage his reputation in the field in which he worked. He called himself a builder, even if he was in reality more of a landlord who simply repaired the properties he owned.

And yet, I thought – and I told him this – that the impact would surely not be all that great. The most local of his properties were at least two hundred miles away and the others more like a thousand. But he didn't see it that way. Why should he, after all?

Anyway, there remained the question of whether there was a gay man hiding at the centre of Paul's being, or whether his thing with me was a one-off aberration: the exception that tested the rule. He'd told me, in the confessional mode that we'd both got into on the day that Portia died, 'There were a couple of things that happened when I was a teenager.' Meaning gay things. But he'd stared straight ahead of him when he said this; he hadn't turned to look into my eyes. Nor did he elaborate. I didn't ask him to. Perhaps he would open up on the subject when we got to Italy. Or perhaps not.

He'd said, 'I'm sorry about the last few days. Not being able to talk to you or see you. Not wanting to, truth be told.' He did look into my eyes at that point and I was glad of that. 'I was confused. I still am. I only knew I couldn't handle meeting you. But Portia seems to have been the paw of fate that drew you back to me.'

I couldn't help smiling at the 'paw of fate'. I said, 'I was confused once, too.'

He looked at me with an expression of surprise in his eyes, but I also saw something hopeful there. 'Were you? About your sexuality, I mean?'

'Yes,' I said simply. 'But it was a very long time ago.'

Perhaps I would open up on the subject when we got to Italy.

When we got to Italy. I hung onto that thought like someone clinging to the end of a rope that dangles over a void. Hand over hand I had to climb it now, or fall, and perish in my fall.

EIGHT

'Your new man looks nice,' Hannah said the next time we shared a shift at the King Billy.

'Don't read too much into what you saw,' I told her.

Now she gave me a look from which I read rather a lot. 'Oh, come on,' she said. 'The body language, the looks you were giving each other. You were holding hands on the table-top at one point.' I hadn't remembered doing that. 'You're obviously completely in love. Both of you.'

Hannah had breezily said, while wrapping cutlery in paper serviettes, what I hadn't yet allowed myself to think. 'It isn't as simple as that,' I said. 'He isn't gay.'

There are some things that women don't do in literature. They don't sweat, and they don't guffaw. But I can't describe the explosive laugh that Hannah gave way to at that moment in any other way. Hannah guffawed. 'Pull the other one,' she said.

'It's true,' I tried to explain. 'He's into women. Heavily.'

'He might well be,' Hannah said. 'But not as heavily as he's into you.'

In spite of myself I was massively cheered on hearing this. I drew a breath. 'Well, we're going to Italy together next week. See what happens there.'

'Italy?' Hannah said. 'How long for?'

'Three weeks,' I said.

'Have you told them here?' She meant had I informed my employers at the pub that I wouldn't be available for work for an extended period.

'Oh,' I said. 'I'd forgotten that. Perhaps I'd better.'

Hannah nodded at that.

Paul and I didn't meet during those next days. He had to go to Cornwall to deal with some maintenance stuff at his cottages there. But we were constantly in touch, by text, email and phone. And remotely together, if that's the right way to put it, we made our travel plans. We decided against driving down. The Jaguar was a fun car but it gobbled the fuel. Driving it to Italy and back would be an expense I could do without. Paul, though his car was ten times more economical than mine, spent much of his life driving to Cornwall and back and liked his holidays to be holidays. We agreed on a compromise: we'd fly to Pisa and rent a car when we got there. See a bit of Tuscany, then head further south. See where we ended up.

Not seeing Paul for nearly a week gave me ample chance to think about him. Too much time, perhaps. (It also gave him time to think about me. More on that shortly.) I found myself trying to make sense of what had happened between us, and of what was happening now, and trying to guess – this the most impossible and the most futile – what the future would hold for the two of us. What it would hold; what it could.

I asked myself if I was in love with Paul. I wasn't sure. I wanted to be in love with him. A year after Graham's death I was suddenly ready to fall in love again; though it was something that would have been unthinkable just six months before. But now I wanted someone to love – anyone, actually – in the same desperate way that empty lungs need air. But was Paul simply a good-looking man I'd had good sex with? Someone likeable but nothing more? Were my feelings for him born merely out of loneliness, and given added strength by the frisson of his heterosexual credentials: the unavailable becoming unexpectedly, teasingly, partially available … just to me?

If you have to ask yourself whether or not you're in love, received wisdom has it, then you are not. I chastened my eager thoughts with that grim truism every time they grew too optimistic: something that happened several times each day. And then I got an email from Paul, written late at night in a hotel room somewhere on the Cornish coast.

My Darling Peter

Gosh, he'd never called me that before!

This is a difficult email for me to write. Especially because I am writing to a more or less professional writer, which I am not.

Now I don't know how to go on...

OK. I take the bull by its horns. I am writing to tell you that I have fallen in love with you. I have only felt like this a couple of times in my life before.

Now I've said it it's a weight off my mind. But I don't know how you're going to react. And I don't know what the consequences to me will be.

I think I better end this email now.

With Love

Paul xxxxx

I sat staring at the screen, rigid with shock. Thoughts, like electric pulses, tore through me. One impulse was to pick up the phone immediately. But what would I say? I probably wouldn't find words at all, but simply cry. Perhaps he'd do the same. Anyway, he'd written those words last night; I was reading them at nine the next morning. He would be out at work, doing repairs perhaps, or negotiating with tenants face to face: those were not things to be interrupted by such a phone-call as mine would be.

I got up and paced the room. Paul had declared himself. He was in love with me. I had to ask myself, now more seriously than before: was I in love with him? The answer came back sheepishly, but it was no answer at all. The answer was that I still wasn't sure.

I made myself some coffee. And then a thought came to me that was reassuring. Things don't have to happen at exactly the same moment between a pair of people who love. I knew this from spending twenty years with Graham. Sometimes he was more in love with me than I was with him, sometimes it was the other way round. But over our twenty years together it had evened out. When he died I was in no doubt that we'd lived in love for twenty years. It was the same with physical love-making. It was very rare for two people to have an orgasm simultaneously. But no-one had ever thought that mattered very much. It made no difference to the fact that the two of you had indeed made love.

So let things take their course, I counselled myself. Take things one day at a time. See what happened when we got to Italy...

Italy was being asked to take on a hell of a lot of responsibility, I realised. I just hoped that it would be up to the task.

One day at a time. Today's challenge would be to answer Paul's email. A tough one, that. I wasn't going to lie to him, just to make things easier in the short term for myself. But who has ever replied to such a tender avowal as Paul's with the announcement that, as they're not sure whether they return the other's love with equal intensity, the probability is that they do not?

I did have other things to do that day. I got them all

done first. It is wonderful how much work you can accomplish while putting off a truly difficult phone-call, letter or email. But then, at seven in the evening, by which time I knew Paul would be aching to hear my reply, I had to sit down at my computer and make a start.

My Darling Paul...

The phone rang. Anything to save me from going on with this email. I answered it. Paul's voice. I might have expected that. Though I wasn't expecting what he said. 'I'm back from Cornwall. Can I come round?'

My heart did some painful gymnastics then. 'Of course,' I said. 'Where...?' I didn't finish the question. He had ended the call.

I glanced around me. I hadn't tidied the house for a week or more. Did I have time to file a few papers? Put the vacuum round? No, I did not. The doorbell rang. Paul must have been parked in sight of the house, looking at the lights in my windows through his windscreen, when he made that call.

I opened the door. He stood outside. Despite his greater height he looked this evening as small as a weasel, and as fragile as a bird. This moment was the mirror of the moment just a week ago when I'd turned up on his doorstep, desperate and vulnerable, to announce the death of my cat. There was only one thing I could say to him now that wouldn't hurt him terribly, hurt him more terribly than he already hurt. I said it. 'I love you, Paul.'

And as I said it I realised that I meant it. I had never meant anything more seriously in my life. I took him in my arms, and he took me in his, and heedless of whether there were neighbours abroad to hear us we rained tears upon each other's cheeks, and sobbed chokingly until our lean frames shook.

We feasted that evening on each other's bodies, and on each other's hearts. We sprawled together on my sofa, sometimes Paul on top and sometimes me. So intimately entwined we were at some points that we literally didn't know which one of us was which. 'Steady, you're crushing my elbow,' one of us would say, and the other would answer, 'Sorry, I thought it was mine.' We found we had two tongues: they both belonged now to both of us. The same went for our four big bollocks and our pair of cocks. As far as the former went we were matched very equally; in respect of the latter, though, not quite. I'm reasonably well endowed, for a guy of my modest size. But Paul, three inches taller than me... Well, I don't need to spell it out.

'I had to come back,' Paul said between mouthfuls of me. 'You didn't reply to my email.'

'I know, I know,' I said. Paul's words were as painful to me as if I'd been made to swallow fish-bones. 'I got it this morning. I imagined you already out at work... And also,' I faltered wretchedly, 'I didn't know what to say.'

'And now?' Paul's nose and chin were tucked in

against mine. The words came out distorted, like those of a ventriloquist.

'I know what to say now,' I said. 'I'll always know what to say from now on. If you'll let me, that is.'

'I'll let you,' Paul said.

'Then I'll say it. I love you till it hurts.'

He stirred uncomfortably amongst me. 'It will hurt,' he said ominously. 'Love always does.'

That bitter truth notwithstanding, we cooked up some pasta for supper and ate it at the table, in the happiest of states, washing it down with a comforting bottle of red wine. Then we went upstairs. The bed was cold when we got into it and Paul was shivering. But I made sure he didn't shiver for very long.

NINE

We were going to fly to Pisa from Gatwick. Nothing should have been easier than for us to get to Gatwick. It was just over thirty miles away as the jet flew, and Paul and I could see the planes descending towards their final approaches from where we lived. On summer weekends I had even watched them circling in the nearest of the holding stacks in the western sky. But the drive to the airport was a different matter. It was over fifty miles by the shortest route, and over sixty if you saved time – and spent more money on petrol – by taking the motorway. As for the train, that took a leisurely run south west along the coast, and actually doubled back on its tracks when it got to Eastbourne, before heading north to the airport.

It became more difficult the more we thought about it, and the more that I understood what was going on in Paul's head. Parking even one of our cars at the airport for three whole weeks would be expensive. We ruled that out. Sharing a taxi all the way would actually make good sense, but Paul vetoed that. We were both known by name as well as sight to all the local taxi drivers, and they knew everybody else. If the two of us were to travel to Gatwick by taxi together, with suitcases in the back, our relationship would become public knowledge as quickly as if we'd written the information on a banner and flown it from the flagpole that crowned Rye church.

The train option... 'We'd need to get to Hastings

station in two separate taxis,' Paul said. Same reason as above.

'Oh for God's sake,' I said, exasperated. Then added facetiously, 'We could always wear stocking masks.' He had the good sense to laugh at that. 'Look,' I said, 'I'll ask Finbar to run us to the station.' Paul knew who Finbar was by now, though he hadn't met him yet. My friend and neighbour who had sold me his Jag. Whom I had deserted in favour of Paul when Portia died. 'He's as discreet as an oyster. He won't talk.'

'Well, if you're sure...' said Paul doubtfully.

'Guaranteed,' I said. 'I have to say, though, that if we continue to spend time together people will eventually find out.'

'Cross that bridge when we come to it, then,' said Paul a bit grimly.

'Italy first,' I said, and to my relief Paul laughed.

Finbar was a big lad of Irish extraction, about the same age as Paul. Like many men of his age group he lived on his own in the wake of a divorce. Finbar would drive us in my car, we had decided. The car had recently been his anyway, and the petrol would be at my expense. We gave him a bottle of wine also, though, by way of thanks. I deliberately sat in the back seat of the Jaguar on the way to the station, so that Paul and Finbar could get to know each other a little in the front. After Finbar had deposited us Paul said, 'He's a handsome chappie.'

'Yes,' I said, half pleased and half surprised by Paul's remark. 'I didn't think you were supposed to notice things like that: straight guy like you.'

'You'd be surprised what I notice,' Paul said, while a teasing smile played around his lips.

Being in love, whether you are fifteen or fifty, involves a most glorious compendium of first times. They follow on from each other as soon as you move away from what has become the comfort zone of the place where you met, and the bed you first shared together. Paul and I had slept together all of the four nights between his return from Cornwall and our departure, arriving at each other's houses after dark in the evening and driving away again before the morning light was in the sky. We didn't see each other during those daytimes; we had work to do and dared not be seen together – at least Paul dared not be seen with me – at either the Harrow or the King Billy when the day's work was finished. Those nights were short but intense. But now we were setting out together into that big adventure of first times.

We hadn't been in a car together before today. Bizarrely, this morning we had travelled in my car which, exceptionally, was being driven by someone else. Never mind, we chalked it up as a first. We had never been in a railway station booking hall before. We watched each other's demeanour at the ticket window carefully, learning from the moment a little more about each other: how we behaved in different situations; who we were.

We'd never been on a train together. But we had plenty of time now to get used to this. Our train edged at a frustrating slowness in and out of platform after platform – there was little more than a mile between each of those many seaside halts. We sat opposite each other, knee to knee. (Because Paul's legs were so long, anyone who sat opposite him on a train would have to sit knee to knee with him, whether they were in love with him or not.) When we ran out of things to say, and of things to point out in the passing South Downs landscape, we gazed happily into each other's eyes and exchanged lovers' smiles.

Never before had we shared the familiar rites of check-in and the vigil of waiting at an airport. The mutual chin-spraying with after-shave in the Duty-Free, which involved so many different brands that the pongs all got indescribably mixed up. The coffee and the croissants at a mind-numbing price. The public taking off and putting on of metal-strapped watches and leather belts. All these things had been my rites of air-passage with Graham for years. They had been stripped from me on his death like epaulettes that denoted an exalted rank. To have them returned to me today – to have them returned to me by Paul – gave me such a wonderful chest-swelling feeling that the tightness hurt.

We'd never before climbed an escalator together. Gatwick gave us our big chance. There's an escalator there so big it could have been a prop in the film

Stairway to Heaven. It climbs you up to a glassed-in bridge so high and broad that airliners taxi nonchalantly beneath you as you cross it. Paul and I rode up together. By standing one step higher than him I could look a little way down into his eyes for the first time ever instead of always up. He smiled up at me. We started to kiss. And didn't stop till we reached the summit, taking no notice of all the other people riding down next to us, who, to their credit, took little notice of us either. It was lovely to be with a Paul who no longer cared about the watching eyes and twittering tongues of two small villages miles away. And, after we'd ridden over the void on the long moving walkway, we kissed again all the way down to the bottom on the other side.

Never before had Paul and I tumbled together into the leather seats of business class, fumbled together for our seat-belt straps, and ended up – of course – groping each other's upper legs.

We took off into a dazzling blue sky in which, on this day in early May, no cloud lurked as far as we could see. I quickly learned that Paul was one of those people who likes to know, when in an aeroplane, exactly what is going on and where he is. 'Undercarriage up,' he noted matter-of-factly, on hearing that regular dull thump a few seconds after take-off, and then proceeded to make guesses about the angles of the wing-flaps. I was fine with that. I was in love with him: that meant I was in love with everything about him, including the fact that he turned into a geek as soon as he boarded a plane.

It was lucky that the day was such a clear one. If Paul

liked to know exactly where he was, then today he had no excuse not to. We crossed the English coast at Brighton, and the French coast at Dieppe – the town's massive harbour that twisted and funnelled its way through the town rendered it unmistakeable – and then, picking up a view of the winding Seine on the right, winged our way towards and then across the sprawl of Paris. The horizon ahead of us grew lumpy after that, then jagged, and became the Alps. Stiff peaks of meringue inched slowly away beneath us, icing sugar blowing occasionally from their tops in hazy wreaths like smoke.

We flew downhill across the plains of northern Italy. Turin, then Genoa. Out across the great bay of the Mediterranean. Then a sharp left turn above the water found us swooping low towards a coastline; minutes later we were on the ground at Pisa.

It's easier to buy things in a foreign language than it is to sell them, and car hire is no exception. We were on the road in no time at all. Paul drove the first leg. To my astonishment he'd privately planned a route away from the airport and memorised it, to the disgruntlement of the temporarily redundant satnav. Eschewing the motorway network and my map-reading skills as well as those of the satnav, he threaded our way along minor roads through scenic hills and forests until we found ourselves beneath a pinnacle of rock, like a landlocked miniature Gibraltar, on which was perched a town called Volterra. 'Time for lunch?' I suggested, and Paul, whose thoughts clearly chimed with mine, swung immediately up onto the corkscrew road that led to the citadel.

You can't just drive into the interiors of Tuscan walled towns. There is someone at the gate who stops you and redirects you to an edge-of-town car park that costs a lot and necessitates a two-hundred metre climb back up. I knew that. Paul either didn't know or else was a superb actor. He drove straight in through the town's medieval arched gate, ignoring the flagging-down gesture of the policeman on duty under the arch. He drove along the ancient main street and parked right outside a café that had taken his fancy at a distance of a hundred yards. We had a pizza each and a glass of red wine. Then we drove out and down the corkscrew hill again. I waved to the gate-guarding policeman as we swept past. He didn't react. I was not only in love with Paul by now. I was also much impressed.

We stopped in a lay-by to have a pee, in a grove of mimosa trees. It was my turn to drive after that. Our road turned boot-lacey. It coiled uphill and down again and became as disorienting as a voyage through the small intestine. And then...

And in the afternoon they came unto a land

In which it seeméd always afternoon.

We had to stop. Across the rolling hills a ghostly sight appeared. The red-brick towers, taller than factory chimneys, of San Gimignano reared as if from underground. How far away did the town of fairy-tale turrets lie? Four miles? Six? It lay, shimmering in the heat-haze, glimmering in the afternoon sun, five hundred years ago in time. We were looking out on a scene of beauty that hadn't changed in half a thousand years. It was a picture of an ideal medieval landscape, the kind depicted in the Psalters and Missals that the monks made all that time ago. It seemed to beckon us.

'Should we go and look at it?' I asked Paul.

'What would we find if we got there?' he asked in reply and, reaching across the gear-lever, caressed my thigh.

'Car-parks and coach-parks?' I hazarded. 'Over-priced cafés and hordes of British and German tourists blocking the pavements and eating ice-creams as they walk?'

Paul nodded. 'Distance lends enchantment. Doesn't everyone say that? Why don't we keep the enchantment? Drive on. And while you do, get your cock out.'

That startled me. I could hardly have imagined the man I met over the bar stools at the Harrow just a month ago would be saying this to me as we drove on a mountain road in Tuscany so shortly afterwards. But he did say it. And I did get my cock out.

Paul did the same. And, in a state of semi-undress most gay teenagers might think twice about, we drove the labyrinthine hill twists through the warmth of an Italian spring afternoon, occasionally backing up to accommodate other drivers on hairpin corners, waving to them with our free hands as with the other two we each fondled the other's warm and furry bits.

'Tell me about Finbar,' Paul said suddenly. That jarred slightly. It seemed strange to want to talk about a third party, especially one whom Paul had barely met, while we were driving through the cypress-studded hills of Tuscany for the first time while playing with each other's exposed and rampant dicks. Never mind. I would do my best.

'I've known him for years,' I said. 'I knew his wife. They married young. Two kids. They've moved away now they're grown up.'

'He must be lonely, then, if he's divorced.'

'They visit him often,' I said. 'And, from the sex point of view he does all right.'

I didn't elaborate. I knew little enough about Finbar's sex life myself, and it would have been disloyal, I thought, to share even that. Paul seemed to realise that: he didn't pursue it. 'What does he do?' he asked.

'He's a vet,' I said. 'Spends his days on farms up to the elbow in cows' gynecological bits.'

'Fun job,' said Paul. 'Still, I guess it pays the bills. Anyway he's a handsome bloke.' This was the second time Paul had mentioned this. 'That mop of brown curls. At his age – what, my age? – with hardly a grey thread in sight.'

'You had a good look while you were in the passenger

seat this morning,' I managed to say with a laugh. I'd thought I was the gay guy who'd taken a fancy to the straight man who was Paul. But was Paul, perhaps, the straight man who had taken a fancy to a man, Finbar, who was even straighter than Paul was? Did that happen to straight men? For all my age and experience I had never encountered it. But I had learnt that there was no end to the surprises and strangenesses of life.

I said, 'Perhaps we'd better tuck our dicks away now.' We were entering the town of Poggibonsi. 'I'll need to concentrate. Besides, we don't want to ejaculate in front of pedestrians while we're stopped at the first set of traffic light.' Paul saw the point. He folded himself away, not without a bit of difficulty, and zipped up. I said, 'Can you do me too?' The car was manual shift. I needed one hand for the wheel and the other for the gear-stick. Paul obliged, very lovingly and very carefully, managing not to impale my rigid member on the teeth of my zip.

Our destination was a tiny town called Pienza. Like Volterra and the other towns around it was perched on a hill in the middle of scenery that had brought travellers to look at it for centuries. We nosed up towards it along a narrow bootlace road, through fields already sun-yellow with rape flower. Here and there stood comfortable-looking farmhouses, red roof-tiles and golden walls shining in the sun, and guarded by tall sharp cypress-trees that, against the vivid yellow of their backgrounds looked almost charcoal-black.

At the top of the climb, a medieval gateway, and a

policeman to guard it. In contrast to Paul, driving into Voltera, I stopped, wound the window down and asked permission to unload our baggage at the hotel before coming back out to park. Permission was granted smilingly, and we inched our way through the pedestrian quarter of this sparkling jewel of a town. When we got out of the car Paul stretched his long legs and arms. He looked about him. 'Better to travel hopefully than to arrive, they say. I don't know, though. Arriving here... With you...'

'Let's get inside,' I said. 'Then I'll give you a fucking kiss.'

TEN

It was like a honeymoon. Of course it was like a honeymoon: it was a honeymoon. Those days at Pienza. That wonderful week.

Pienza is romantic in the extreme. In this hilltop village, inhabited as long ago as the age of the Etruscans, and by the Middle Ages known as Corsignano, was born in 1404 a child called Enea Silvio Piccolomino. He loved the view from his hilltop birthplace, and never forgot it. He became a scholar and a writer: he was the author of an erotic novel, among other things, and some reams of erotic verse. He grew more serious as he grew older and became a priest, and then a bishop. His work took him as far afield as Basel, Newcastle and Edinburgh. In 1458 he was elected Pope. He reigned until his death, six years later, under the name of Pius II.

As Pope he returned to his birthplace of Corsignano, and built a palace and a cathedral there. The village grew in stature, and became Pienza, taking its name from its now famous son, *Papa Pio*. From his palace's south-facing loggia a wonderful view of the Orcia valley rolls out like a tapestry depicting the Garden of Eden. Pope Pius would stand or sit here and marvel at it. And five and a half centuries later, so did Paul and I.

But Franco Zefirelli had got here in between. He used the papal palace for the interior scenes of the Capulets' palace in his film of Romeo and Juliet. He used the

town's square also. The builders of the square had built
it to a wonderful harmonious design, including steps and
a sloping ramp, golden stone walls that caught the sun
and made magic shadows at morning and evening, and
with an elaborate town well in one corner, next to the
palace of the pope. It was as though they had built the
hub of the little town in the full knowledge or
expectation that somebody would one day invent the
medium of cinema.

The tiny town and its associations fitted Paul and me
like gloves. We might be middle-aged rather than in our
teens as Romeo and Juliet were, but we were as much in
love as any two teenagers could be – we knew this
because we'd been teenagers ourselves once – and, like
the more famous couple, were conscious that we had
obstacles to face. But we were on our honeymoon and
we chose to ignore all difficulties for now.

Our hotel was like the papal palace in miniature. It
was actually only two doors away (just the cathedral was
wedged in between) and was yet another medieval
building. It had once been a Franciscan monastery – or
friary, to be strictly correct. Our bedroom was high-
ceilinged and massively chestnut-beamed. A beautifully
decorated ante-room led into it. This had an elaborately
constructed fireplace and a painted ceiling, dating from
the renaissance. Though in theory we shared this
chamber with other guests, who would pass through
occasionally on their way to their rooms, we used this as
our private sitting-room, and would snuggle on the
leather sofa there after the town had closed up, enjoying

a night-cap as we did so, when we felt it was still too early to go to bed. From this position we would disentangle ourselves just enough, from time to time, to wave other bed-bound guests a smug goodnight.

In the daytimes we drove around the surrounding countryside. We visited the hilltop wine towns of Montalcino and Montepulciano. Not only their two names were confusingly alike. In both places we parked at the foot of the town and took the bus up to the pinnacle. Then we walked slowly down, enjoying a church or a cathedral, a sunny medieval square, and stopping off for a wine-tasting outside a bar among the winding corkscrew streets. But somehow our memories got blurred. After two days it was no longer possible to remember which of the rival-twin wine towns was which.

We wore shorts during the day, of course. Curiously, although you may have slept naked with a boyfriend for a few weeks, and spent time in the same state walking around the bedroom and even draped over the living-room chairs, there is something very special about walking around outside with him in the sunshine, admiring that special shape of the part of him, comprising knees and calf muscles, that's framed between the hems of his shorts'-legs above and his concertina-ed white socks below, while knowing that at the same time he's admiring you in exactly the same new way. Paul's legs were longer and ganglier than mine. But the muscles in them were wiry and well-toned. I was proud to be in the company of his shorts-clad legs. I knew, and was very happy, that he was proud to be in the company of mine.

In the evenings, back in Pienza, we sat outside, by the town wall, looking again across the valley below, to where the mysterious lonely hill of Radicofani crowned the distant horizon with its eerie solitary tower. From here we watched the sun go down, setting fire to the deep blue sky, and saw Venus, like a silver pin, and the dark flickering bats, come out. Radiating away from our high perch were little high-walled alleyways. The Via dell'Amore, the Via della Fortuna, and the Via del Bacio. The Street of Love, the Street of Luck, the Street of the Kiss. We thought we couldn't have come to a more appropriate place.

There was a time, not long ago, when a holiday meant a complete break from work. But email and the mobile phone have put an end to that. Even I had to check my emails daily during our stay. Availability checks for my services as a role-player in medical training. And I had the occasional paragraph to write, or query to answer, on a gay website. But Paul spent three of four times longer than I had to, doing this... Well, that was the price he had to pay for being rich. He needed to check that rents were being paid. To answer tenants' queries. Deal with maintenance problems. He had to stay on top of his job...

'Why don't you do it all through agencies?' I asked him one morning when we were sitting outside the breakfast room, me basking in the sun and the view from the garden (same view of course), Paul busy on his lap-top.

He looked up at me. 'And have them rip me off every minute of every day?'

'Save yourself the hassle,' I said. 'You don't need all this. Let them rip you off a bit. Does it matter? You'd still be mega-rich.' We knew each other well enough now to have exchanged the secrets of our bank accounts and finances. The small secrets of my finances. The big secrets of his.

He said, 'That's not the point.'

I didn't pursue it. I didn't say, 'You'll give yourself a heart attack.' I'd already said that once. I was learning another thing about him: Paul loathed to delegate.

A day or two earlier I'd asked him how he got on with emails and calls that came through from tenants and local powers-that-be in either German, Portuguese or Spanish. 'I manage,' he'd told me. 'They tend to be fairly same-ish, and I've picked up enough at least to understand. Writing back can be a bit tough. Katie used to help.' Katie was the name of his ex. She'd been a holiday company courier when younger, he told me, and was operational in all of those three languages.

'You were lucky,' I'd said. 'But now you've got lucky again. I can get by in Spanish and German. Well enough to compose an email or speak on the phone at any rate. Any help you need... Well,' I shrugged. 'You know who to ask.'

He beamed at me. Seemed genuinely delighted. 'I did pick the right man for my homosexual adventure, didn't I? That's brilliant, mate.' Then he paused and said a bit bashfully, 'I don't suppose you do Portuguese as well?'

I made a face. 'Sorry. That's where I fail the test. Duarte was my first dip into Portuguese waters, and that didn't really last. Still,' I went on – and to this day I don't know what made me say this – 'Finbar's good at Portuguese. He had a Portuguese wife.'

'No, really?' Paul said. Then, 'We should have brought him with us. In case anything came up.' I looked at him carefully, checking to see that he was joking. He turned towards me and laughed, so apparently he was.

We had what we now considered 'our' seats, outside a small bar just behind the parapet of the town wall, from where we could look hundreds of feet down upon the road that wound its way up to the town's 'back gate' beneath us, and miles across to Radicofani, eerie and alone on the distant horizon. As we sat there each evening in the twilight warmth, sipping a glass of Brunello di Montalcino, it was not only the stars that came out one by one to silver the sky, and not only the little pipistrelle bats and the big noctules, but we ourselves – little by little revealing to each other the inner workings of our minds and the hidden wells of our hearts.

'You don't have many friends, I think,' Paul said one time.

'No,' I said. 'Graham and I were very self-sufficient. We didn't need other people much. It wasn't till he died that I realised how far out on a limb I'd climbed.'

Paul reached for my hand across the little outdoor table and clasped it. There were a couple of other tables with customers sitting at them. None of those seemed to care. Though I did.

'Until God or fate sawed off the branch you were sitting on.' Paul said this quietly, but he gave the hand of mine that he was holding a powerful squeeze.

I said, 'But now I've got you.'

'And Finbar, of course,' Paul said. 'You've got Finbar.'

'Well, yes,' I said, slightly disconcerted. 'Yes, I've still got Finbar.' My mind went back to the days after Graham's death when most human company was as abrasive to me as the touch of a dogfish's thorny hide and I shrank away from it as from something I could not bear. At that time Finbar was the only person I felt comfortable with. And it was in Finbar's company one summer evening, when just the two of us were sharing a bottle of wine in his garden, surrounded by nodding columbine flowers, that I discovered, for the first time since I lost Graham, that I could be happy – if only for this fleeting moment – once again. I told Paul this story now.

'Finbar is good for you,' Paul said gently. 'I hope he'll be good for me too.'

I wasn't sure quite what Paul meant by that. I said, 'Because you don't have many friends either?'

'That's right. For twenty years all my friends were Katie's and my friends. When we split up… well, it was like she got custody of the friends.' That made me smile, even though what he had told me was desperately sad. I leaned forward across the table, half standing up to do so, and kissed him on the lips. A kiss which he returned. When I'd sat back down in my seat, Paul pointed to the street sign just a few yards away. *Via dell'Amore*. 'Ti amo, Peter,' he said softly. 'You see, I'm making great strides in Italian.'

I said, 'Ti amo, Paul.'

We travelled short distances into our tapestry landscape. It was like being able to drive deep into a painting by Bellini or Uccello and be at one with it. We explored the rambling stone village of San Quírico and the Roman baths at Bagno Vignoni. We hiked one day the short but down-and-up road to Monticchiello through vines and olive groves and found ourselves in the tiniest and most fairytale hill village of all. But our eyes strayed always to the far horizon on the southern edge of the valley where the distant tower of Radicofani pointed into the sky like a finger accusing God. Its brooding presence on the edge of our little world haunted us. 'It's like something from The Lord of the Rings,' I said.

Paul agreed. 'The tower in the valley of Isengard,' he

said decisively. 'It's Saruman's tower of Orthanc.'

The name of Radicofani was written on every signpost. Even the name was haunting, like the name of any place that has the word *far* – in this case simply *fa* – in it. 'We'll have to go there,' I said.

Paul gave me one of his odd looks. 'Are you sure we should?' he said.

I remembered what he had said when I suggested visiting San Gimignano. 'You're thinking, distance lends enchantment, again, aren't you,' I said. 'That by going there we'll spoil the magic, break the spell.'

'Something like that,' Paul said, nodding. 'But also, my father used to say, "Leave something for the next time." The idea was to have a reason to come back again.'

That stirred something inside me. 'Would you like to come back here again? With me again?'

'Yes,' Paul said, looking into my eyes seriously.

I met his gaze. 'Me too,' I said. We both knew how big this moment was. We'd just told each other in a few cryptic yet powerful words that we thought we had a future together, that we weren't simply about *now*.

We made an effort to communicate in Italian, though it was a language that neither of us had ever learnt to speak. But we loved the sound of it and – thanks to the fact that we both knew the odd phrase or two from opera – found it easier to pronounce than German or French. With the help of an old phrase-book I'd brought along, and with Paul having Google Translate on his phone (he used it for those tricky emails to Portugal and Spain) we managed to order drinks and food, ask directions when driving and, with luck, understand the answers people gave us.

We even began to converse, haltingly and with frequent recourse to hand gesture, with the staff in the restaurants we went to for our evening meals. Especially in the one we found the friendliest: a simple pizza place. Not until our last night in Pienza did they ask us which country we came from, though. *Inghilterra,* we said.

'You should have said before!' said the son of the house, a young man I found I rather fancied, though I hadn't told Paul this. He exploded into an English that was anything but beginner-standard. 'I thought you were German or French or something. Most Brits and Americans don't speak a word of anything else.'

I was a bit taken aback to hear him speaking like this: a waiter in a pizza restaurant in a hill village in the middle of Tuscany. 'Where did you get your English from?' I asked, trying to keep the astonishment out of my voice.

'London,' he answered. 'I lived there for two years. Shared a flat at the Elephant and Castle.' It gave me a weird feeling to hear him saying that.

And so we chatted, the three of us, for half an hour or more. Where were we going on to next? our new friend wanted to know when we eventually got up to leave.

'Rome,' Paul said.

'Good luck with car parking, then.' And the young man, whose name was Salvatore, proceeded to give us some handy tips on the subject. Then he leaned down closer to us. 'If you are looking for gay action – man-on-man, you know – then Trastevere is the place to look.' We thanked him for that too, before we all said goodnight.

As we walked back through the narrow, lamp-lit streets Paul said, 'He was a bit tasty, that one.'

I stopped and looked at him in mock-surprise. 'I can see I'll have to watch you,' I said. 'I didn't know you noticed things like that.'

'I notice everything, remember,' Paul countered.

'You're also a little bit gayer than I used to think.'

I felt Paul's arm come round my waist and draw me into him. 'I might be a little bit gayer than even I used to think.'

ELEVEN

Paul looked up from his lap-top, turning his gaze to me with a puzzled frown. 'There's something odd going on,' he said.

'How do you mean, odd?' I said. We were sitting one last time in the garden of our hotel after breakfast, before driving off towards Rome, in the sunshine and in front of that incomparable view.

'People not paying their rent. If that counts as odd.'

'In the annals of human history it's not unusual,' I said.

'Ha-ha,' said Paul. 'There was a batch of credits that should have appeared in the last couple of days. Sometimes they come a day late. But this time it's three days.'

'Maybe...' I didn't know what I was going to say. Which was just as well, since I didn't get a chance to say it.

'It's all Portugal. Everything's been rolling in from Spain and Cornwall very nicely, but Portugal's just suddenly stopped.'

'Are the banks over there having a problem, do you think?' I was interested, obviously, and even concerned. I wanted to appear business-savvy as well.

'I wondered that. I've just been checking on financial news sites. Not a peep.'

'So what do you think?' I began to worry, selfishly, that he would need to do something – like spend a morning on the phone – and that we wouldn't be able to get out on the road.

'I'm not sure,' he said. 'It could hardly be a mass withholding of rent, surely? I mean it's not as if they all speak the same language, let alone all know each other.'

I thought for a second. 'Have they been complaining a lot lately? I mean, about the rent, state of the properties, terms... I don't know...'

'No more than all tenants complain about everything – always,' Paul said casually.

'How can you find out?' I asked.

'Email them all,' he said. 'Text them. Phone them up.' He sighed his exasperation. 'That'll take time.'

'It's OK,' I said. 'We're not in any hurry. They won't chuck us out of the garden. I can clear our room...'

'OK. Email first. Some of them are Germans – and I really ought to do it in Portuguese as well.'

I only get about one very bright idea a year. Luckily this year's came to me at precisely that moment. 'Dictate what you want to say. I'll translate it into German, if it isn't pages long. And I'll email it to Finbar and with luck he can send it back in Portuguese. We'll get it done in…' I tailed off. It would still take time. Especially if my email found Finbar up to the armpit inside a cow. But I was rewarded with a bright smile of relief from Paul. I smiled back. I think we were both delighted at the thought of working together to iron out a difficulty that one of us had encountered. Lying behind that quiet new delight was a feeling that neither of us tried to put into words: it was the idea of the two of us being able jointly to surmount any obstacle that life placed in front of us; that individually, separately, we might be small and frail and fallible, but that together we were invincible and could conquer the world.

I phoned Finbar immediately. He was at work, but answered straight away. As soon as my email arrived, he promised, he would translate Paul's what-are-you-playing-at email and send the result back. He hoped that, despite Paul's current little worry, we had been having a good time. By now Paul had drafted what he wanted to say. We sent the words to Finbar and then I set to and did my German version.

While I did this Paul had a look at the advertisements for his properties that he had placed on the websites he used. They didn't look quite right, he said, looking up from his laptop and giving me an anxious look across the garden table. Some of the details had been slightly changed. There was a misspelling in one of them. 'They've been tampered with,' he said.

He contacted the websites at once – they promised replies in a few hours. By this time Finbar's translation into Portuguese had arrived, and Paul was able to send off his by now tri-lingual email, while I fetched us both a coffee from inside the hotel. At last Paul closed his laptop, heaved a very spontaneous sigh and said, 'Can't do any more for the moment. Let's get out on the road.'

When you are in Italy you discover just how literally you can take the saying that all roads lead to Rome. Even in remotest countryside the name of the capital can be found on almost every signpost. Our way would not be difficult to find.

The road took us nearer to Radicofani than we had expected, and then past the great Lake of Bolsena, which flashed at us from its almost circular depression among the surrounding hills with all the brilliance of a diamond ring. Then across country to Montalto di Castro, from where the Via Aurélia swept us down the coast towards the south. We arrived, beneath a blue springtime sky, in the warmth of mid-afternoon.

Paul had chosen a hotel that was shoe-horned into the picturesque maze of streets that make up the Trastevere district, just across the river from the central ancient sites and just the other side of the Janiculum Hill from St Peter's Cathedral and the Vatican. Paul was the wealthier of the two of us: I had been happy to let him choose our hotel. Arriving there, finding our room with its splendid views, and the neighbouring streets attractively sequinned with restaurants and bars, should have been an idyllic experience, a moment to savour. It was marred, though, by the anxiety that gnawed at Paul:

his need to find out what was going wrong with business interests a thousand miles away; to track down the apparently vanished income that – if you wanted to look at it this way – should be paying for our honeymoon-like days in Rome.

So we spent most of the rest of the afternoon in our hotel bedroom: Paul sitting on the double bed busy with lap-top and phone, trying to sort his problems out, and me, now that I'd done my bit as a translator, and having roped in Finbar additionally in the same role, unable to help further for the moment and not doing very much except make occasional suggestions that were never any use. Oh, all right, I did at one point write a postcard to Hannah at the King Billy. I stuck to the traditional banalities that the genre requires. We were having a lovely time; the weather was very good. I said nothing of the fact that Paul was worried sick that someone might have stolen his identity, or part of it. Nor that his sexual identity – whose heterosexual essence I had proclaimed loudly last time Hannah and I had spoken about it – was no longer where he had always thought it was. His identity as a straight guy had got lost somehow in recent weeks. I knew that. It was I who had stolen it.

I stopped Paul eventually. 'It's seven o'clock,' I said. 'We've had nothing to eat since breakfast and my stomach's beginning to think someone's cut my throat. I'm taking you out. Now.'

To my secret relief Paul accepted the suggestion gracefully. Having secured his agreement in this matter I now found myself able to persuade him to leave not only his lap-top but also his mobile phone in the hotel room safe while we went out. 'The lights are going out all over Europe,' I told him. 'At least they are in everyone's offices. You can't do anything more till morning comes.' I was rather hoping that he and I might manage to do something along those lines in the intervening time. We'd had enjoyed quite exuberant sex every day while we'd been at Pienza, usually during the afternoons, in the course of siestas that never quite turned into sleep.

We walked to the bank of the Tiber and found a bar from whose terrace we gazed across the eternally flowing river at the half-hidden treasures, the half-ruined buildings and columns, of the ancient city. When John Burgon wrote of a city "half as old as time" he was not thinking of Rome. But he easily might have been.

We dived back into the labyrinth of streets between the river bank and our hotel and selected a restaurant to eat at. With the cloud of worry that hung over us we knew we weren't going to be out on the town, foot-loose and carefree, doing the bars and clubs of Trastevere till the early hours. But at least we could console ourselves with the one thing that can make Italians happy when they are sad. We could indulge in the thing that brings a glow to Italian boys' faces when their girlfriends aren't around; we could give ourselves over to the experience that tides the Italian teenager over from the *mama* years to the *figa fresca* times to come. The fact of life that is spelled out in a mere five letters in every language in the world. Pasta is its name.

We had tortelloni parcels that were stuffed with

chicken, walnuts and cheese, served with a cream sauce and drizzled with truffle oil. That was followed by saltimbocca – a scallop of veal, wrapped in Parma ham and leaves of sage, then pan fried. A chocolate dessert that was as light as foam... Actually, it was mostly made of foam. A bottle of wine... But what made the meal memorable, for me at least, was not to be found on the menu or in our mouths. It was something Paul did after the meal was ended.

While we sat savouring our desserts two men in their early twenties came in and sat at the bar, where they each ordered a small beer. Paul could see them easily. I had to turn my head to do so, though I did this readily enough from time to time when Paul told me to. 'Are they gay?' we asked each other, asked ourselves, as middle-aged male couples always do when in the proximity of a pair of younger men who seem to like each other, and also look cute. The two young men sat sideways on to the bar, balancing atop high stools. Their knees almost touched.

'I think they are,' I said in an expert tone. I was three years older than Paul and had been gay for much longer than he had (ha-ha) and so I was expected to know.

'Ah, now I'm sure of it,' Paul said suddenly. This announcement coincided with an urgent need of mine to turn and look at the 'specials' menu board chalked up behind the bar and above the two young guys' heads. They had now each taken the other's hand and were playing with each other's fingers as they rested their wrists on their respective knees. I tried not to notice this as I scrutinised the high and far-off list of antipasti, like someone who has enjoyed his meal so much that he wants to begin it all over again.

I turned back to Paul. 'I think that's very nice,' I said. Meanwhile the image of the two of them, hands clasped as they sat at the bar and looking into each other's eyes, remained engraved on my own retinas and would not go away. In such a way had Paul and I sat at the bar of the Harrow more than once, though we'd been a long way from feeling able to clasp hands. It was a kind of behaviour that, even in 2014, was probably less acceptable in much of Rome than in the pubs around Rye. And yet there are lots of things you feel able to do when you're six hundred miles from home that prove a bit of a social stumbling block when you're two hundred times nearer to your front door. For this latter reason I felt able to reach across the tablecloth in search of Paul's long strong fingers, and for the same reason those long fingers had no hesitation in very firmly, very publicly, clasping mine.

It was time to pay the bill. Paul got up and walked to the counter to do it. I watched him from where I sat. This time I had a better excuse to turn towards the bar. I saw Paul get his wallet out, explain what he wanted to do. Then I saw him point to each of the two young men and to the beer pump they were sitting by. Saw the bartender's nod of comprehension, and his quick indication to the younger guys that they had just been bought a drink.

At that moment a large man approached the counter

and stood between Paul and the two young men. Their nods and surprised smiles of thanks were thus blocked from Paul's view, and so, without a second's hesitation, they transferred those smiles and nods to me. Paul and I had come to a particular conclusion about the two young men: now it seemed that they had clocked us too, and fingered us as gay.

We all four exchanged further smiles and little waves as Paul and I made our eventual way to the door. In the street outside Paul said, 'I wanted to let them know it's OK for them to be who they are. That if it's OK for us, then it's fine for them too. That we are what they can become one day.'

'I think that was lovely of you, Paul,' I said. I felt myself choking up. This was happening more and more often as I shared his company. The beauty of him that was evident in his outward appearance also ran very deep.

'I wanted them to know that they're not the only gays in the village,' Paul went on. I could hear a determined, clenched tone coming into his voice.

'Pretty big village, Rome,' I said, to lighten my own intensity as much as his. I knew that Rome wasn't really the village he had in mind. Think Icklesham. Think Rye.

There were several things about what Paul had just done that stirred my heart. One was the simple generosity of the gesture. The next was Paul's readiness to consider a possible emotional need in two strangers at a time when he was preoccupied with serious business troubles. And then there was something else. What he had done, what he had said, marked a very big step along a journey that was Paul's own, and one I couldn't really share: the road to his coming out to himself as a gay man. In the now dusk-filled street outside the restaurant I put my arm around Paul and hugged him, and he knew exactly why.

We walked and talked along the floodlit walls, and among the spring-green trees, that lined the Tiber's banks, marvelling at the weightless arches of the white bridges that straddled the current. Back at our hotel eventually, we permitted each other to check our emails… That is to say, I permitted Paul to check his. None had come in that were related to his business worries. 'No news is good news,' I attempted to say brightly, but I knew that in this case it was certainly not good news. Paul didn't draw attention to the daftness of my utterance by dignifying it with a reply. He just raised an eyebrow and screwed up his face a little on one side. He did that from time, for all sorts of reasons, which I had now learned to read. It was yet another little trait of his that I was coming to love.

Only after that did Paul check his left-behind phone. There was nothing. Except a voice message, asking how things were going – from Finbar.

TWELVE

During this tour of Italy we were having our first experience of sleeping together as a matter of course night after night. For the moment, at least, we had said goodbye to the experience of occasional nights grabbed like precious objects from the chaotic flood of life. We now had the comfort that established couples have: the comfort of knowing that each day would end with the two of us in bed together, snuggled up and, one way or another, making love.

But this night was different. Once we got into bed we held each other with the desperation of two people adrift and in fear of drowning in that chaotic flood. Neither of us made a move towards sex; neither of us was hard (yes, we did check that at least); we both wanted simply to hold and be held by the other throughout that night; and somehow that was more wonderful than anything else could have been.

But the morning began early. With phone-calls to banks, messages from websites, and a few replies to the trilingual email we'd sent out the day before. Although Paul actually made his first call of the day not to any of these but to Finbar, to thank him for his concern, and I was impressed by this demonstration of Paul's thoughtfulness. When that call was finished Paul turned to me and said, 'He's offered to give us any more help we need. He's actually got a few days off work at the moment, so he's got the time.'

'Well, that's very kind of him,' I said, trying not to sound nettled by the fact that Finbar, who was my best straight friend, was now making his offers of assistance directly to Paul rather than channelling them through me ... and, come to think of it, it was Paul, not me, whom Finbar had phoned last night... 'but I can't really see what more he could do.'

Paul put his head on one side in that way of his that I was coming to find extremely attractive and said, 'Well, he does happen to be fluent in Portuguese...' He left it at that and started in on his morning's on-line oakum picking. Happily the hotel had a rooftop terrace where we could sit in the sun with cups of coffee that followed each other like beads on a rosary chain; we didn't have to remain confined to our bedroom. After a little time of trying to make myself useful to Paul and finding I couldn't be I asked him if he'd mind if I went out for a walk for an hour. If he needed me back in a hurry he was to call me on my phone.

Because I wanted to see the main sights with Paul I didn't take myself across the river into the ancient centre of the capital, the *centro storico*. Nor did I pre-empt the visit that we planned to make jointly to St Peter's and the Vatican. Instead I decided I would take my solitary ramble up the Janiculum Hill.

Rome was famously built on seven hills, but the Janiculum was not one of them. It lay outside the small area that constituted the city of Rome in ancient times. It was, however, easily accessible from our hotel. A short walk along the Via Garibaldi, then into the Vicolo del

Cedro, brought me to the foot of a series of flights of steps that led to the top of the ridge of the Janiculum. Here stood the church of San Pietro in Montorio, built on the spot where it was believed that St Peter, first of the apostles and – according to Catholic theology – the rock on which Christ built his church, was crucified. Crucified upside down at his own insistence, as he considered himself unworthy to be put to death in the same way as his master: i.e. the right way up. I was never a Catholic but I have always taken a bit of an interest in St Peter. After all, ever since birth I've shared his name.

Roaming further along the ridge of the Janiculum I found myself in a peaceful, wooded area of high ground, networked by small paths. Dotted about along the pathways were statues of the heroes of the Risorgimento, as well as strategically placed bench seats. The views from these were enchanting. The whole of the city lay spread below and in front of me, across the Tiber's looping coils. There lay the Pantheon, there – more difficult to pick out among the surrounding rooftops – was the Coliseum. The massive bulk of the Castel Sant'Angelo loomed up in the distance and there too was Bramante's great dome crowning St Peter's, against a backdrop of church spires and towers too numerous for me to even guess their names.

The central, highest part of the hill was wonderfully empty of human activity and noise. The air was scented with the resinous exhalations of the pine trees and hummed with insect buzz. I hoped the air was not too empty, though. I didn't want to be out of signal range, should Paul need me and decide to call my phone. After lingering a little while in this peaceful spot I retraced my steps and went back down to Trastevere, checking for messages once I found myself again among the streets. There were no messages, about which I was rather relieved.

I went straight up to the hotel roof terrace. There was Paul, still in shorts, still with lap-top open on his knees, the sight of him producing that tiny electric jolt in the chest that reminds lovers the world over that they are still in love. When he saw me he put the lap-top down and stood up. He walked towards me and, two seconds later, took me in his arms.

'Something's happened,' I said, alarmed suddenly.

He gave me a kiss, then disentangled himself. 'Yes and no,' he said. 'I'm afraid we need to leave Rome today...' My heart sank. '...And fly to Portugal.' I don't think there's a word for what my heart did then – sort of pleased but aghast at the same time. Then, in astonishment, I heard Paul say, 'Finbar's going to meet us there.'

There is no word to describe how I felt about that either. 'Finbar?' I queried. 'You've been talking to Finbar? You didn't think to phone me?'

'You were out on a wander,' Paul said. He tried not to sound sheepish as he said this but was only partially successful. I was getting to know him well.

'I had my phone,' I said. 'I deliberately went to a high place,' I pointed across the rooftops to the wooded crest of the Janiculum just half a mile away, 'so I could get a signal if you phoned.'

'Well, how was I to know that?' Paul said. 'You didn't tell me.'

'You could have...' I began. I heard myself, and stopped. 'Sorry, darling,' I said. 'Let's not argue.'

Paul took me in his arms again.

We drove to the airport, still wearing shorts, as soon as we'd packed. Paul had dealt with the reception staff, checking out. Whether he'd get any money back I didn't know. I didn't ask him. It wasn't the right moment.

Paul explained the situation piecemeal as we went along. Someone claiming to be Paul had changed the bank and other contact details that he used for collecting his rents in the Algarve. He now needed to present himself in person at a lawyer's office in Albufeira, and also at the police station there, to re-establish his identity. He needed a fair number of paper documents with him when he did this. 'But you haven't got those,' I butted in. 'Your passport, yes, but...'

'That's where Finbar comes in,' he said. 'He's going to collect the paperwork and bring it out.'

'But how?' I asked. 'He doesn't have keys to your

house…'

'No, but a neighbour of mine does. I've called her and told her to expect him. I've told him what he needs to pick up and where to find it. With any luck he'll be joining us late tonight.'

I bit back my thoughts. That Finbar was my best friend, not Paul's, and how dared Paul muscle in on Finbar in this way without involving me as intermediary? They weren't worthy thoughts, I knew. But still…

There were no direct flights from Rome to Faro, the airport of the Algarve: the airport that was handiest for the properties that Paul owned between Albufeira and Portimao. We had to fly to Lisbon, then either drive the hundred and fifty miles or take another short flight. 'I didn't want to drive all that way today,' Paul said. 'And you seem OK with flying. So I booked the connecting flight from Lisbon to Faro. Hope that's OK.' I thought it was fine.

Actually it was quite spectacular. The day was fine and clear. We headed out to sea at once, across the sparkling Mediterranean, and within minutes the islands of Corsica and Sardinia had materialised ahead. We flew through the narrow gap between them, the Strait of Bonifacio. Neither of us had a brilliant view today: we'd booked very late and had to count ourselves lucky to have got aisle seats, though separated by the gangway, in the same row. At the moment of passing between the two islands I stood up in my seat in order to get a better view.

'Sit down, you're rocking the plane,' complained Paul.

'No way,' I said. 'How many times in my life am I going to fly from Rome to Lisbon? How many times am I going to look out at Sardinia below me on one side and Corsica on the other?'

'You're right,' Paul said, giving one of his lop-sided grins. He undid his seat belt and stood up too. Together we shared the view on both sides of us: the mountainous, hedgehog-backed island of Corsica to starboard, the gentler-hilled sprawl of Sardinia to port; two dark jewels set – Shakespeare's words, not mine – in a silver sea. We held hands across the gangway at one moment: it's easy to stand up and be counted when you love and know that you are loved in return.

A flight passes quickly when there are landmarks underneath. The Balearics lining themselves up for inspection on the left-hand side. Menorca, Mallorca and Ibiza in a row. (They'd have been in alphabetical order coming the other way.) The coast of Spain at Valencia. Sierras sawing their toothed way upward through the lion-skin plains. Far away to the south the snowy cap of Mulhacen swimming into focus out of the distant mountain blue. At last descending along the Guadiana valley, a swoop around the huge-bridged Tagus estuary, and the kiss of tyre on tarmac, and we were on the ground in Portugal.

Romantics like myself cling to the idea that when you change planes in a fabulous city like Lisbon you may have time to slip out and visit the city centre during the hour or so between your two flights. We know of course that this won't be the case but even so...

It wasn't the case. Obviously. By the time we'd cleared customs and passports the time was nearly come for us to go to the boarding gate. We had just a jewel-like moment in which to establish a greeting bond with Portugal. A real greeting in my case; I'd never been here before. Paul steered me towards a coffee shop from which, through the distorting glass of a passenger walkway, the baked tarmac of the airport runways could be seen beyond palm trees. And there we had a tiny and bracingly fierce coffee, and ate a *pastel de nata* – my first on Portuguese soil. A pastel de nata is nothing more or less than a custard tart. But it's made the Portuguese way, to a secret recipe handed down by nuns since the Middle Ages. Portuguese ex-pats dream of this delicacy just as Italians lie awake thinking of pasta. As I ate mine and as Paul ate his, I could understand why.

The last leg of the journey was short and sweet. There were views of the Atlantic and the south-westernmost point of Europe at Cape St Vincent, then we were over the mini-mountain of Monchique, the coastal lagoons of Faro, and down. We hired a car, and Paul drove us up into the hills.

One of his properties lay empty, as it happened, and

that was where we were going to stay. At least Paul knew where it was. We wound our way up a dirt track as the sun went down behind the Atlantic hills. Below us a beautiful wooded valley dropped away as we climbed. Gates opened automatically at our approach and then Paul was opening up the house.

Two things struck me at once as we went inside. The place was wonderfully spacious and beautifully furnished; picture windows gave onto the valley below and looking down there you could see lights were coming on. That was one thing. The other thing was that it was freezing cold.

Paul flicked the switch that started the central heating, though naturally that had no immediate effect. So we went out into the big terraced garden and dragged in logs from the woodpile there while below us in the dark ravine the nightingales began tremulously to sing. Soon a fire was burning in the big hearth in the living room. The logs were orange wood, and they scented the whole house with the smell of the fruit. We didn't have time to sit down and enjoy the scented warmth, though. My phone rang. Finbar had arrived at the airport. Could we go down and meet him? Of course we could. I was absurdly, disproportionately, pleased that he'd chosen to contact us this time via my phone rather than Paul's.

I suppose I could have let Paul go back to the airport and collect Finbar while I stayed put and cooked us all a meal. But I'm just human, not an angel: like anybody else in my position I insisted on going back to Faro with him.

Coming through the automatic doors from customs, looking about him in an unfamiliar place, looking a little lost and bewildered so far from his comfort zone, Finbar looked absolutely lovely in his sudden vulnerability. My heart performed a little skip. It wasn't supposed to do that now for anyone except Paul. I hadn't wanted it to do that when Finbar appeared. It shouldn't have done it. But it did.

I called out, 'Finbar, over here.' He looked round and grinned his relief at seeing us. The three of us walked towards each other. Spontaneously I gave my friend a hug. Then Finbar hugged Paul too. I had vaguely imagined that the emotional choreography between the three of us might get complicated over the next few days. Now I knew for certain that it would.

'Car's just outside.' Paul said this in a business-like way. He took the keys from his pocket and waved them in Finbar's face as if he thought the announcement might not be believed. Though, come to think of it, that little signal with the car keys is the one we all make when we want to show that we're the one in charge.

We whizzed back along the motorway: it took only a few minutes. Then before tackling the winding track-way up the hill from the village, Paul pulled into the car-park of a restaurant he knew. In the Algarve you eat fish if you have any sense about you, and so that was what we did. I sat alongside Paul as we ate, and Finbar, with whom I'd never shared a restaurant meal before, sat opposite us. He began to relax as he tucked into his sea-bass and our shared bottle of white wine. His blue eyes began to smile. 'It's very good to see you both,' he said, nodding. 'Three of us together. We'll get this sorted. Everything'll go just fine.'

'Hope so,' said Paul, bright all of a sudden.

I said, 'Hmm.'

THIRTEEN

The house was warm when we got back. Paul had switched on the central heating before we went out. And although the log fire had died down in our absence it proved easy to resurrect. It had also aromatised the whole house with the scent of oranges.

What do three straight men do when they find themselves sharing a house together in a sudden and unexpected intimacy? They reach for the beer cans or the wine bottles to take the awkwardness out of the situation. There were no cans of beer in our kitchen as it happened, but there were a few bottles of wine, and we got stuck into those pretty immediately. We were going to behave like three straight men, it seemed. At least for the moment.

We hadn't long been settled around the scented fire, glasses of red wine in hand, when Finbar said, looking at Paul sharply, 'I've seen you before, of course. I thought that when I drove you to the station last week, but I couldn't remember a context. Of course, though, I used to see you in the Harrow. Went there with my wife sometimes. And you'd be there with... I guess... yours.'

'Girlfriend,' said Paul. 'We split up.'

'Sorry,' said Finbar. 'I mean, I'd rather guessed you had.' He shot a meaningful glance back at me, then back at Paul again, then back at me. That glance of his seemed to ricochet like a billiard ball. Perhaps his thoughts were doing likewise. 'But my wife and I got divorced a year or two back.'

'I knew that,' said Paul quietly.

I put in, 'Sorry, but it's the sort of thing that friends do tell other friends.' I could have said *that lovers tell other friends*, but I didn't want to rub Finbar's nose in anything.

'So how...?' Finbar made a very expansive shrugging gesture and opened his blue eyes very wide. There was no need for any more words to complete his question.

I said, 'Because life's a strange thing, and human nature more complicated than anyone will ever get to the bottom of.' I looked at Paul as I said this and was reassured by his firm nod of agreement.

Finbar grinned. 'Sure. I'd go along with that. But I really meant the juicy details, if I'm allowed to know them.' A look appeared on his face then that showed he thought he'd gone too far. 'Shut me up if I'm being nosey.'

Between us Paul and I told the story of our meeting by chance in the Harrow. Haltingly we dredged up the story of the night that Paul had had dinner with me and had drunk too much to drive home... We didn't go into more detail than that. The knowing smiles that played about Finbar's mouth told us we didn't need to.

'Then Portia died,' volunteered Paul to my surprise. It gave me a jolt to hear him remember her name and speak it. 'And everything seemed to change gear.'

'I got this most wonderful email...' Now I thought perhaps it was I who had gone too far. I looked shyly at Paul and was rewarded by a look from him that was so happy and bright that it might almost have had tears in it. 'And I suggested on the spur of the moment that we should go on holiday...'

'There've been times in my life when I thought I might be gay,' I heard Finbar say. Heard the words, which seemed to wing their way across the room italicised, almost with disbelief.

For over a year now I had fantasised about going on holiday with Finbar, travelling with him to southern Europe. I had tried not to fantasise about his coming out with the sentence he had just uttered. But now both these things had come to pass. Yet not at all in the way I'd wanted them. I was on my honeymoon with Paul, and wanted him all to myself. Fond as I was of Finbar, I didn't want him here with us at this precise moment. I certainly would have preferred him not to be here at Paul's invitation rather than my own. And the last thing I would have wished was to hear him announce that he had, or had had, gay leanings – while getting slightly drunk in the company of Paul.

Life has a cruel way of timetabling its agenda for us. A year ago, to have found myself snug in front of a fire in a lovely house on the Algarve coast with a bottle of wine, and Finbar for company, and Finbar telling me he thought he might be just a little bit gay... Well, that would have been a situation to die for. I would have been in heaven. But as things were now...

'You'll need to explain that,' I heard Paul say, as he got up to refill Finbar's glass. Oh please, not right now, I thought.

But Finbar heeded Paul's words rather than my merely telepathic output. 'There was a boy at veterinary college,' I heard Finbar say. 'I realised in my second year he had a bit of a crush on me. I guess I found that flattering.'

'Mmm,' murmured Paul, sounding interested, meaning, go on.

'We used to go drinking together, in a group, you understand: guys and girls together.' Paul nodded. So did I. Even I knew that experience. 'One evening there was just the two of us ended up together. We found ourselves walking back through the streets to his place for a nightcap or a coffee. It was the first time I'd been there. The thing is,' he paused for a significant second, 'the thing is, I realised as we walked along together that I was up for anything that might happen between us that evening. Well, within reason, of course.' In spite of myself I felt myself getting excited. I could visualise, inhabit, the scene almost too easily, and a delicious tingle was running up and down my back and arms. 'When we got back to his place there was no-one else in. He poured us both a whisky and we sat together on the sofa, just like with a boy and a girl...' He stopped. 'Sorry, I didn't mean to be crass. I mean, like any two...'

'Just get on with the story,' I said, and shot him a mischievous look. 'We've all been there.'

'Anyway, he put one hand on my thigh, a bit timidly – which was hardly surprising, he was quite a lot smaller than me. But to my surprise – and perhaps I felt a bit ashamed at the time and afterwards, sorry guys – I found I rather liked having his hand there, and I put my own hand on his thigh too. I still remember how very hot it felt. Then he kissed me on the cheek, again quite timidly, but I didn't rebuff him and he got bolder and went for my lips.' Finbar mugged an awkward grin and shrugged again. 'Well, guys, what was I going to do? I kissed him back, and suddenly there I was, a lad of nineteen, for the first time in my life snogging another guy. After a while we broke off and drew slightly apart on the sofa. Both of us unsure what was going to happen next...'

'And?' I prompted, and heard Paul come out with the same word at the same time.

'And one of his housemates came in. So it was just as well we'd separated and were sitting slightly apart on the sofa. But of course we felt hugely compromised, and we must have both blushed and looked as guilty as hell. I know we both had hards-on, though they might not have been spotted by the chap who came in...'

'Hards-on, not hard-ons,' I couldn't help saying. 'That sounds very literary.'

'I'm well-read, like all Irish guys,' Finbar said. 'James Joyce and all.'

'Anyway, what happened?' asked Paul, sounding ever so slightly peeved that I'd interrupted. 'Did it go further?'

'No, it never did,' said Finbar, shaking his head, and I thought I sensed real regret. 'Not that night (we just finished our whiskies quickly and I left) and never again. Just one of those things.'

'One of those things,' echoed Paul. And he got up again and refilled our three glasses. And then I was startled to hear him say, 'You said there were *times* in your life... Not just one time...' He let it hang there, but his meaning was clear. If Finbar had more to tell then Paul wanted to hear it. Now.

Finbar sighed faintly, as if the rest of this was going to be harder to relate than the first episode had been. Perhaps he was regretting having started this hare in the first place. But then he looked at his replenished glass of ruby liquid – which looked horribly like a bribe, I thought now – and set off again. 'The second time was after I was married,' he said. He looked firmly into my eyes and then into Paul's. 'The second and last time, by the way.'

In case he was afraid that Paul or I – or both of us – might want tonight to be the third? I had to wonder. Though I wasn't going to wonder it out loud. 'You don't have to tell us if you don't want,' I said. Though the subtext was as plain to Finbar as it was to Paul and me. I was as eager now to hear this story as was Paul.

'Again it concerned a vet,' Finbar said. Then he shifted in his chair. 'Oh hey, I've never found myself confessing this before. Not to anyone. You'll have to forgive me if it comes out a bit … unrehearsed.'

Paul and I made sympathetic humming noises and nodded our encouragement.

'I'd been at a conference in the west country. Cirencester or somewhere. I was on the train going back to London, and sitting opposite someone who'd been at the conference with me. We hadn't had much to do with each other but I'd found myself thinking he was probably rather nice. It seemed like he thought the same about me, because we got chatting very easily on the train. Obviously we mentioned where we were travelling to. I told him I'd be getting off the train at Reading, and changing to go back down to Sussex via Tonbridge.

'Reading was where he lived, he told me. With his wife and two kids. Then we talked about places we'd been to abroad. He told me about a conference he'd been to in Bordeaux. A couple of the other guys that time had been gay, he said. He stopped at that point and watched my face, I noticed, to see how this was going down. I must have given some sign of encouragement, I suppose, because he went on to say that they had taken him out one night to a gay bar. They'd had a fun time, he said but – in his words, "Nothing happened." But – he went on – the next night he had gone back to the bar on his own and...

'"And this time something did?" I said. I don't know why I came out with that. Perhaps I was remembering that time at college. I know I found myself getting a bit turned on by the story he was telling me. He gave me a rather inscrutable smile and said rather quickly that, yes, something had happened. But he clammed up rather quickly then. It was left to me to say something. I said something along the lines of, well, I was married but something had happened to me once, but I left it at that, and we talked of other things.

'Then we both got off the train at Reading. We were about to say goodbye on the platform. But we were actually near the gents' toilet and he saw the sign for it and said, "Actually I need a piss." And I said something like, so did I. And we both went in together and stood alongside. And guess what? I looked at his and he looked at mine and we were both, well... And actually so much so that we weren't able to go.

'Anyway, he suddenly said, "I don't suppose you could spare an hour?" He said the kids wouldn't be home from school for an hour or more, and he didn't live far away. We ended up taking a taxi, which he paid for. The next thing, we were in his kids' bedroom and taking our clothes off. I couldn't believe this was happening. I'd never done this before in my life. We got down on the floor... Well, you don't need the details...' (No, we didn't. All the same, they would have been nice.) 'Enough to say we sixty-nined each other, though we came in each other's hands, not mouths, and after that we crowded into the toilet together and had what was by now a pretty desperate piss.'

'Still naked, I suppose?' I asked. For someone who wasn't going to give all the details Finbar had been pretty generous with them. I just wanted that last one so that I could join the dots.

'Yep,' Finbar said. 'Then we got dressed very quickly because his kids were coming home, and I walked back to the station and caught my train home. I've never seen him, or heard from him, again.' He exhaled a sudden gust of air. 'Hey, I've never told anybody that. 'You will keep it to your...?'

'Obviously,' said Paul, for both of us.

'Anyway,' Finbar said, 'that's my gay life history. All of it. What about yours?' He took a sip of wine and looked roguishly from Paul to me.

'Oh God,' I said. My head was swimming with alcohol by now. I really wanted to get to bed. 'Mine would take too long. And we've got a big day tomorrow.' I looked at my watch. 'It's already nearly two o'clock. Look, tomorrow evening I'll tell anyone who still wants to hear it. But maybe Paul?' I looked at my new boyfriend, and wondered whether, much as I wanted to hear the details of his early homosexual fumblings, I wanted to hear them now, this late at night, and in the company of Finbar.

But Paul shook his head and said, 'Nah. Not tonight. Tomorrow, yeah, though. If we're all still alive.' He stood up, to top the glasses up one last time, and I just had time to clock that he had a semi-erection before he used his forearm very quickly to smooth it down. I looked at Finbar. There was a significant bulge in his jeans also. As for mine – well, I need hardly say.

We got businesslike after that. The beds were made up in all three bedrooms. Paul made it clear at once which one would be his and mine, and gave Finbar the choice of the other two. One was right next door to ours, the other separated it from it by a bathroom, and Finbar very tactfully chose the latter. At least we wouldn't have to listen to each other's fartings and other eventual noises during the night. Then we said goodnight. Paul and I each gave Finbar an almost pointedly brief hug, and then went to our room.

'That was all a bit unexpected,' I said, when Paul and I were undressing. We still liked to watch each other while we were doing this. It was nice that we hadn't grown out of that.

'What? That straight guys might have a bit a gay past hidden about their persons?' Paul said this nicely, with a sweet smile, and a cock that wavered in and out of erection mode.

'No,' I said. 'I do know that. I've had adventures with straight guys before – which I'll tell you about some other day. It's just that... Finbar, you know...'

'C'mon,' Paul said, taking charge as, from time to time, he liked to. 'Bathroom. Toothpaste-time.'

But Finbar's presence and his stories had left their marks on us. After we'd cleaned our teeth and done all the rest of it, and had tumbled into bed, we were both excited enough to try to fuck each other. Though too drunk actually to succeed, either way around. The next thing we knew, our door was opening and Finbar, dressed in nothing but the tiniest, tightest pair of white shorts, was walking towards our bed, a mug of tea in each hand.

'Come on, you pair of stayabed shirtlifters,' he said. 'Move yourselves. It's nine o'clock. We're due at the lawyers at ten thirty.'

FOURTEEN

I had never seen Finbar in shorts before. Certainly not in a pair like the ones he was wearing this morning, which left almost nothing to the imagination. All right, you couldn't actually tell whether he was circumcised or not, but you could still see that he had a pretty big one. At this time of the morning at any rate.

He and I had actually had a conversation about shorts once, last summer. Finbar would often see me in shorts, at home, in my garden, and even when I went round to his. 'I never see you in shorts, though,' I said casually on that occasion. 'Well, I couldn't wear them around you,' he said. He was joking, of course, but even so I couldn't find the breath to quip back.

But now here he was, wearing so little as to suggest he was making some kind of statement. Or perhaps for Finbar it was a case of 'safety in numbers' where gay men were concerned. Paul and I were making a counter-statement of course. Simply by being in bed together. And very obviously naked, since we both sat up, letting the duvet fall back almost too revealingly as we reached out for our morning mugs of tea with groans of thanks.

It was business as usual after that, though. We all showered – though Paul and I did at least share this experience, as had become our habit – and got decently dressed. Regrettably decently, actually, since the sun was shining and the morning was warm. But there was no question of wearing shorts when we headed out. We were not tourists here but on an extremely serious mission, and our seriousness would have to be demonstrated from the first moment of our encounters with both the lawyer and the police.

We drove off at once, promising ourselves a quick coffee and *pastel de nata* in the sunshine as soon as we'd managed to park in Albufeira, if there were a few minutes to spare before our appointment with the lawyer.

We were lucky: there were a few minutes and we savoured them sitting at a pavement café, knowing these might be our last moments of comfortable relaxation for a considerable time. The sands run slowly in police stations and lawyers' offices. Then, fortified by our coffee, we walked round the block to the offices of the lawyer who had been recommended to Paul by an Algarve residents' protection website. We were shown into a waiting room and there we waited. And waited.

At last the lawyer appeared, a slender white-haired man with the demeanour of an undertaker. Paul stood up, gave his name, and immediately introduced Finbar, in simple Portuguese, as his translator. They all shook hands. The lawyer then looked at me curiously and looked back at Finbar, asking who I was. I understood Finbar's words easily. He presented me as Paul's civil partner. At that moment I blessed Finbar for being here for Paul, for being here for *us*, and regretted my mean and jealous thoughts of yesterday. We all need friends, and I had no business resenting Paul's reaching out to

Finbar in a moment of crisis…

The next moments didn't go quite so well. The lawyer looked gravely at Finbar. I was Paul's civil partner, then, was I, as in British law? Well… In that case, did we have the paperwork to prove who I was? (This, even before we got onto the question of who Paul was.) Had we brought the partnership licence with us? Er, no, said Finbar. The lawyer made it clear that there was no place for me at the meeting that was about to take place, and suggested that, for the sake of everything's running smoothly as the day progressed, when it came to the visit to the police station it would simplify things if I just didn't show my face at all.

I was shaken by all this. I'd have written *outraged,* but I wasn't feeling in a very strong position and I certainly wasn't going to argue or bluster, or do anything that might create a difficulty for Paul – or Finbar for that matter. Paul turned to me, with a very upset expression on his face and said, sorry but…

'It's fine,' I said. 'I'll take myself off to a beach somewhere for the morning. By bus. Phone me when you're done at the police station and we'll meet back up. You'll have the car. Come and get me.'

Paul said, 'Go to Galé,' and gave me the number of the bus I needed. Then he gave me a quiet, but in the circumstances defiant, kiss and I turned and left.

To my surprise the bus stop proved easy to find and the bus was as quick in coming along as the lawyer had been slow. It took me along a narrow lane beside the coast and deposited me at Galé, which turned out to be a sedate and peaceful beach village, boasting some handsome houses behind high walls with security gates, a couple of swish hotels, and a collection of beach bars and restaurants, all nestling cosily among sand dunes and pine trees.

I wasn't dressed for the beach. Well, not exactly. I was wearing neatly pressed fawn chinos, a blue open-necked shirt and deck shoes with dark socks – as a courtesy to the Portuguese legal system I had eschewed my usual white ones. Rather than sit down on the sand – staring out to sea and worrying helplessly about what was going on at the lawyer's office and the police station – I decided to walk along it.

Beaches are longer than you think. I had once walked along a beach on Majorca, heading for the cathedral of Palma, which appeared to be just around the next corner, jutting into the bay on a little rocky outcrop. I hadn't realised quite how massive the cathedral was. The walk took nearly all day.

Either I hadn't learnt the lesson of that occasion, or had forgotten it. A little way along the sandy crescent ahead of me the white buildings of the next village or small town lay. Or rather, stood. Some of them looked like the tower blocks of modern hotels. They shimmered in the mid-morning heat on the rim of the blue-filled saucer of the bay. I took off my shoes and socks and stuffed them into the pockets of my chinos, one on each side. Then I walked towards my mirage-like objective along the edge of the teasing waves. If a phone summons came from Paul I could simply cut away from the sea and cross the dunes to the coast road which ran along behind them, and wait like a hitch-hiker to be picked up there.

I walked for nearly an hour. The buildings ahead of me had grown a little bigger but not very much. I needed a piss. I could have done it where I was, at the edge of the waves, but there were people dotted about in the vicinity, so I decided instead to make my way into the dunes and do it there.

The dunes turned out to be quite vast in terms of area. The coast road had evidently had to take a biggish turn away from the beach to allow for the space they took up. But at least there was space, and it seemed quite deserted. Sheltered by towers of grass-grown sand on all sides I unzipped and started to do what I had come here for.

But no sooner had I begun than I discovered that the dunes were anything but empty of people. First one head appeared over the top of a low heap of sand, and then another. Further off a figure stood up, tall, proud, naked – and even at the distance he was from me – unmistakeably male.

There was no point attempting to stop what I was doing, now that my audience had already got an eyeful. I decided there was nothing for it but to keep calm and carry on. Even so… Before I had finished a man of perhaps thirty had materialised in front of me. He wasn't naked. He was dressed in a thong. Though only just. He pulled it aside and let his own dick hang out and water the sand in front of me. By the time he'd finished he was seriously stiff. By that time I too had finished, and so was I.

Sometimes temptation disappears of its own accord, before you've had a chance to decide whether you'll give way to it or not. The young man stuffed himself away (the gesture was more symbolic than effectual) and turned away towards the sea.

My phone rang at that moment. I had to take one shoe out of my pocket in order to answer it. I didn't have time to put my stiff dick away.

'Hi,' I said, in that giveaway tone that infects the voice of every man who gets caught with his cock out.

'Hi, darling. You all right?' was Paul's immediate, concerned, response.

'Fine,' I managed to say. An elderly man, stark naked except for a backpack, was making his way towards me along a path in the sand I had hardly realised was there. 'How are you?'

'We're done. At least for the morning. Where are you?' In spite of the hideous complexity of the moment I registered the *we*. We being Paul and Finbar. It hurt. 'I have to appear before a magistrate to have everything confirmed. And… Hell, it doesn't matter right now. I want to come and get you.'

I was standing in the centre of the path. I hadn't realised that. The elderly man, who was small, rotund and smiley, was almost upon me. He had a small, pert cock that was circumcised. Either that or he'd peeled his foreskin back in order to show it off better. I tried not to pay it too much attention. 'I'm in some dunes,' I said. 'West of Galé. Nearer the next place. Place with hotels.'

'Bloody hell,' said Paul. 'You walked all the way to Praia Grande? You're in the middle of the biggest gay cruising ground in the Algarve. Did you realise that?'

The elderly man smiled broadly at me and, as he passed, without stopping, gave my protruding cock a squeeze. 'Get off,' I said in English.

'What?' said Paul.

'A bloke just grabbed my dick,' I said. 'I'll explain.'

'I hope so,' said Paul, though in a mirthful tone, for which I was grateful. 'Do you want to walk across the dunes towards the road, and we'll pick you up there?' He paused for a second. 'Unless you've unfinished business you need to pursue.'

'No unfinished business, I assure you' I said. 'I stumbled into this place by accident.'

'We'll drive over now. When you hit the road just stay where you find yourself. We'll drive up and down slowly until we spot you.'

Again that *we* that was Finbar and Paul. I was no

position to protest, though. 'I love you,' I said, and just had time to hear Paul echo the sentiment before I ended the call. I put the phone back in my shoe, and put the whole lot back in my pocket. Then I calmly replaced my now flaccid cock inside my chinos.

Keeping the sea behind me I wound my way inland through the dunes, zigzagging this way and that rather than climbing endlessly up and down. As I passed a series of men of all ages, sizes and shapes, sitting or lying naked on towels, some in the shade of parasols, one or two rather fetchingly clad in T-shirts above their exposed cocks and balls, I had time to reflect that being under-dressed or over-dressed for the situation in which you find yourself is a purely relative affair.

At last I found the road. Sand-blown from the dunes, it was difficult to spot until I was almost upon it. Then I waited patiently, waited for the car that contained my new boyfriend Paul and his new straight mate Finbar. The new *us*. I tried hard not to think of it in this way. But still I did.

One hire car looks much like another. Unless you've memorised the number-plate. Which I had not. But when one car pulled up across the road, with two men in the front seats I had enough wits about me to know this was my lift.

Finbar had the grace and the good sense to hop out of the front passenger seat and install himself in the back. I got into the front seat in Finbar's place and found the seat attractively, yet disconcertingly hot.

'How did you end up here?' Paul asked.

'How did you know about it?' I batted back.

'Maybe that's all for later,' Paul said, and I was happy enough with that. 'Thing is,' Paul went on, 'I have to assert my right to be who I am – which has now been ratified, if I've got the right word, by the lawyer and the police – in a court of law this afternoon. To set the whole thing in stone. They couldn't find a slot in Albufeira or Portimao or Loulé, so we have to drive to Silves.'

'Silves?' I said. 'Where the hell is that?'

I wasn't too pleased to hear Finbar chirp up with the answer. 'It's the old capital of the Algarve. A little way inland. Beautiful cathedral and everything. If you have to spend time there on your own.'

Fuck you, Finbar, I thought.

I made up my mind I would make the best of it. It wasn't much more than a dozen miles to Silves, and the road ran gently upwards through sun-washed countryside. Low hills sprouted olive groves and vineyards in lively alternation and on both sides of us hoopoes, bee-eaters and cuckoos flew from tree to tree. Silves appeared surprisingly soon, its cathedral dome a wonderfully Portuguese collage of blue and gold rising from the horizon to meet a sky to match.

Paul, driving, took charge as we drove into town. 'I know a great place for lunch.' Was there ever a phrase that said "I'm taking charge" more happily than that?

It was a small restaurant near the cathedral, to which few tourists would ever percolate. It was clad with blue Portuguese frieze-tiles on the outside and when we went inside we found it clad with blue frieze-tiles there too. For starters we had the freshest prawns I'd ever tasted, and for mains a chicken stew. When you've been lucky enough to have a wonderful starter the main course often comes over as so-so. With no disrespect to this particular restaurant, and simply because the starter was so excellent, the chicken stew did come into the category of so-so. But the chips that accompanied it were pretty good.

So was the cathedral, which I was left to wander around on my own. I had walked up with Paul and Finbar to the door of the *Tribunal de Comarca* but had to leave them there to get on with the business of the day without my help, and walk back down the hill. In the hot midday sunshine I walked up another one to find the cathedral. A blend of Moorish and Gothic, it was a building that unexpectedly flooded with light when I walked into it and found myself in the middle of a petrified palm grove of arches and stone columns. I sat down on a bench halfway down the aisle. And just as unexpectedly, my eyes flooded suddenly with tears.

FIFTEEN

Coming out of the cathedral I was confronted with the sight of Paul and Finbar walking towards me side by side. Paul smiled and said, 'Let's get a beer.' We made for the nearest café.

'One of those things that look horribly difficult beforehand but then the difficulty melts away, and when you look back...' I knew exactly what Finbar meant when he said that, but I'd have preferred to hear the good news from Paul. However Finbar went on, 'He had to swear on oath that he is who he says he is, and that was that. Took just a few minutes.'

'Well, that's been the easy part,' Paul said, sounding a bit less upbeat than Finbar. 'It means the police will start a criminal investigation into where my money's gone and who's got it. No guarantee I'll ever get it back. But I've still got to persuade the individual tenants to change their standing orders back to my account again.'

Finbar came in. 'And taking no chances, we're going to call on them all individually. In person. It's only nine houses after all. Give ourselves two days.'

This made good sense. But I was less than happy to be told all this by Finbar. OK, Finbar had been with Paul when they emerged from the court house, and Paul would naturally share his immediate plans with the person who was with him at the time. But all the same... 'Who's we?' I challenged Finbar. *'We're* going to call on them.'

Finbar looked slightly taken aback. 'Well… Sorry, I didn't mean… I mean, I could help with any translation into Portuguese. And if there's German speakers, then you, obviously…' He tailed off awkwardly. He looked towards Paul. 'Up to Paul, really. Whatever Paul wants.'

Paul said evenly, 'I'd like you both with me when I do the house calls. Not just for those reasons. Nice to have some moral support.'

I got a mental picture then of the three of us going from house to house, knocking on all the doors. They'd take us for Jehovah's Witnesses, I thought.

'Starting tomorrow,' I said firmly. 'Right now I'm taking you home for a nap.' I reached across the table and took Paul's hand as I said this, to make it absolutely clear who I was talking to. It seemed that our bedroom was the only place where I could have Paul to myself these days. Finbar could have a nap in his own room if he wanted to, or sit in the garden, or go for a walk, or play with himself. I wasn't too fussed.

Paul seemed to like that idea. He gave my hand a squeeze and nodded and smiled, all without turning to look at Finbar, and that pleased me a lot. We finished our beer, walked back to where we'd parked the car – Silves was one of the easiest district capitals to park in that I'd ever come across – and drove back through the olive-studded hills to the beautiful house on the hillside that I was coming to think of as home.

It isn't really a siesta unless you take all your clothes off, and so that was what Paul and I now did, in the privacy of our bedroom. We hadn't made love – or not properly at any rate – for three days now: not since Paul's troubles had started, while we were still in Tuscany. We made up for that now, while through the open window came the distant calls of the hoopoes and orioles that moved among the trees in the ravine below. I could live here very happily, I thought. With Paul.

Later we drove down to the beach at Galé, enjoying a pre-dinner drink outside a little shack of a bar while looking at the evening-glassy sea. Because of where we were our minds – all three of them, I know – went back to my experience of the morning, when I had walked along the beach from here towards the town I now knew was called Armaçao, and what occurred on the way. It was Finbar who brought the subject up, though. Mischievously, I thought.

'How did you know about the place Peter found himself this morning?' he said to Paul. 'He asked you that; you said you'd tell us later. I think we deserve to be told.' Finbar sat back in his chair, an amused smile on his handsome face, waiting for what Paul would say.

'Well, it's a bit early in the evening for the kind of stories you told us last night,' Paul said. He looked around to see if there was anyone in earshot who looked as though they might understand English. There wasn't anyone. He drew himself up in his chair a bit self-importantly, breathed in through his nose and said, 'But if you want, and because you came clean about a bit of gay stuff in your own past, I suppose I ought to do the same.' He paused and took a gulp of beer. 'It was about eight years ago, I think. Soon after I inherited the properties down here. I was out here on my own, doing a few repairs and stuff. And I did more or less what you did.' He looked at me as he said *you* and gave me one of his lop-sided grins, a self-deprecating one this time. 'I hadn't heard of Praia Grande's reputation in gay circles. I drove down to the beach a little west of here and walked along – like you did – thinking to walk into Armaçao de Pera. After a time I noticed that I'd left the family groups behind, and that the beach was sprinkled, although very... What's the word?'

'Sparsely?' I suggested, in my role as nearly professional writer.

'Sprinkled sparsely, yes,' said Paul, nodding gratefully. (Herbs now came unfortunately to mind.) 'Sprinkled sparsely with men. No women. And if I got close enough to any of them I couldn't help noticing they were naked. One or two had wandered into the water. There were two middle aged guys splashing each other. Bollock naked.'

'And you? You were wearing...?' Finbar asked, sounding as interested as I was. But showing it rather too obviously, I thought.

'I was wearing shorts. Like these, only shorter.' He gestured to the brief khaki pair he was wearing now.

Those shorts of yesteryear must indeed have been short.
'I'd left my top and my shoes in the car. So, yes, just
shorts.'

'Anyway, when I got to the bit where the dunes are, I
saw a man standing on top of one of them. He had a
hard-on. I hadn't seen that many men with hard-ons.' He
stopped and looked at Finbar, remembering something.
'Sorry. Hards-on, Mr Joyce.

'OK, now this really is confession time. I have to
admit I got curious at this point and – if I'm honest,
aroused...'

Um, I thought. *I've known you for weeks now and
you've never trotted out any stories about gay things in
your past...* I rather wished that Paul were telling me this
story as a bed-time confidence, not blurting it out to both
Finbar and me without discriminating between the two
of us. However, I let him carry on.

'I walked into the dunes to see what was going on
there. I saw men, of all ages, lying naked on beach
towels, or else wandering about, strutting their stuff. I
didn't see anybody doing anything with anybody else,
though. Then, quite unexpectedly, I came over the brow
of a little dune and there lay a guy of my own age,
naked, in a little dip in the ground, right at my feet. He
had his eyes closed, but he must have sensed my
presence. He started to play with himself.'

'Was he stiff?' I couldn't help but ask.

'Not at first,' Paul said. 'He was simply squeezing it a

bit and batting it back and forth between his fingers. OK…' Paul mugged a sheepish grin. 'I did get turned on. It was a long time since I'd seen anyone doing that.' (How long? I couldn't help wondering. And when had been the last time?) 'I looked closely at his face as well as his stiffening dick. I could sort of see that his eyes were very slightly open and he was watching me closely through his eyelashes. I reached inside my shorts, and I saw his dick twitch and stiffen up a bit. So did mine at that point. OK, I thought, I'd found my way here by accident, but now I was here…'

'Might as well be hung for a sheep as a lamb,' put in Finbar conversationally.

All this talk of dicks hardening up inside shorts was having an effect inside my own shorts. I was pretty sure, though I tried not to peer too obviously, that the same was happening with the other two.

'OK, I may as well tell you. I unzipped my shorts then and let them fall. They ended up round my ankles. I let the guy have a good clear look at my dick. It was now completely stiff. By then, so was his. He started to masturbate properly, and so did I. The next bit took no time at all. A moment later I'd come onto the sand, and into my dropped shorts. Seconds after that he did the same, turning on his side to hit the sand rather than mess his belly.' Paul stopped and shrugged. 'Well, that's all there was to it. I pulled up my shorts and walked off, back towards the sea. The bloke stayed lying there. Neither of us spoke. Not even a smile.'

I had to say what I said next, cheesy though it was. 'Sex has got better since then, darling. You even get a smile.'

I got a smile from him as a reward for that, for which I was glad. But I was still a bit shocked to hear Paul coming out with such a story in front of Finbar when he'd never till now talked like that when in private with me. Perhaps it had something to do with the euphoria he must be feeling as a result of his success today. Retrieving his identity, if not yet his money. There was a massive sense of relief about him this afternoon. Shared by Finbar and me.

'That was worth hearing,' said Finbar in a mischievous tone of voice. 'So much so that I won't be able to stand up for a few minutes. Perhaps we'd better have another beer.' He waved towards the distant waiter, and did a mime that meant *three more*. With any luck, I thought, by the time the beers arrived at the table our shorts would look presentable again.

'Anyway, Peter,' Finbar resumed, 'we haven't heard your stories yet. You've heard both of ours.'

'I don't think we've heard all of Paul's yet, either,' I said. 'But I'll let that go for now. As for mine, well, there'd be rather a lot of them. I wouldn't know where to start. Unless you want my heterosexual adventures, of course, in which case the story would be over in a flash.'

'I think we're rather in the mood for gay stories,' Finbar said, which amused me but slightly worried me at the same time.

'Later, then. When we're around the fire tonight.' But what I'd just said also worried me. Three of us, around the fire and drinking before bed. Finbar feeling horny, perhaps... I tried to imagine the three of us in bed together. It was a surprisingly easy thing to do. I didn't want a threesome with Finbar. At least, I thought I didn't... How much about ourselves do any of us really know?

The beers arrived and I, for one, still had a bit of a hard-on. I couldn't speak for the other two.

We had dinner at the same restaurant we'd been to the night before. How quickly a routine becomes established. It was only my second visit to this restaurant, and the same went for Finbar, yet the waiters now greeted us by name and I had the feeling, as I looked again at the now familiar menu, that this was *our* place: somewhere we came to every night. We three musketeers. I looked across the table at Finbar as he studied the dishes and obligingly translated the Portuguese. He looked very lovely sitting there, close to me and close to Paul. It was true that I'd had moments of being irritated by him in the last two days. They were moments born out of jealousy, and envy of his easy recent familiarity with my new partner. But I was just as fond of him as I'd always been. I was in love with Paul, and only Paul. Yet in the depths of my heart I also felt love for Finbar.

I still fancied him rotten too.

I drove back up the track. We tumbled home and lit the fire and opened a bottle of red wine. Three hunky boys at the end of our forties or – all right, in my case, touching fifty. We sat around the fire, which was blazing orange and scenting the room with orange zest and fruit. Still in our shorts. And yes, it was very clear, it hung in the air like an aerosol spray of testosterone, that the three of us all fancied one another. The only thing we didn't know at that moment was whether we would all end up tonight in the same bed.

'Peter,' Finbar called across to me, lounging back on his bit of the sofa and supping red, 'the time has come. Your story, please.'

I'd been thinking about this as I drove us all back through the dark. Which of my many stories should I go public with tonight? The first time I wanked off with another chap? The first time I got fucked, when I was seventeen? The first time I fucked another guy – had to wait for that – when I was twenty-one? I drew the line at my first night with Graham. I might tell Paul about that one day, at a moment of the deepest intimacy, but I wasn't going to share it on a night like this, a night of bawdy chatter with two guys I was getting horny with and who were getting horny about each other and about me.

'Give me a moment,' I said, 'and I'll tell you the story of your gay dreams.' This drew titters from the other two. I'd never heard either Paul or Finbar titter before. I didn't know they knew how to do it, actually. Could this have anything to do with me? 'I just need to check my email.'

A routine thing. I flicked through on my phone. Then something caught my eye.

Dear Peter

A reminder that you are booked on Friday May 23rd at...

'Oh fuck,' I said.

'What?' asked Paul.

'I'd forgotten something. I thought I'd cleared the decks before we went to Italy. I've got a medical training thing... Shit! Today's Wednesday. It's on Friday in London...'

'Can't you just cancel?' suggested Finbar, lounging back on the sofa, his handsome legs splayed – displayed – in his very short shorts.

'I could,' I said. 'But I can't. First, it wouldn't be fair. Second, I'd never work again. It's an acting job in its own small way. Actors duck out of work... They never work again. It'll cost me more than the whole fee to travel back to London and back out here. But I've got to do it anyway.'

'Yes,' said Paul, supportively and wonderfully. 'You've got to go. We'll sort you a flight for the morning.' He got up, took the two paces to where I was, and kissed me and cuddled me on the sofa. 'Then you come back to me. I'll pay your fare. But we'll do all that tomorrow. Internet in the morning. Then we'll get you to the airport.'

'You've got your house calls to make,' I said.

'Don't be silly,' said Paul, and kissed me again. 'House calls can wait. We've got a few days for that. Got to get you sorted first.'

I fucking love you, Paul, I wanted to say. But I couldn't quite do it with Finbar there.

SIXTEEN

I was collecting the return halves of plane tickets. Pisa to London, Faro to Rome via Lisbon, and now I was getting a return from Faro to – of all the inconvenient places – Luton. I felt like someone who finds himself opening brackets in a piece of writing, then opening up another set inside, without closing the first, and so on. Come to think of it, that wasn't a bad metaphor for life in general.

I had a window seat, and the day was clear, so I had spectacular views most of the way. But I couldn't enjoy them properly. I wanted Paul next to me, spouting information about wing-flap angles and God knew what else. In the past few weeks he had been poured into my life as if from a bottle of something magical, and by now he filled the whole of it. Without him I was as empty as I'd been when Graham died. But at least I would be going to back to him in two days' time.

Or I hoped I would.

Yesterday evening we had been rather blown off course by the shock we'd got from my summons back to Blighty. I hadn't got round to telling the tales of my youthful gay experiences, and there had certainly been no question of the three of us ending up all together in one bed. We had killed two bottles of red wine between us, and talked of many things, but despite our remaining in shorts and with our bare legs ostentatiously spread, draped across our respective sofas, the sexual static that had been building up all day had vanished, dissipated by the lightning bolt of that email I'd had.

In the morning I had protested that I could find my own way to the airport by taxi: I didn't want to delay Paul on his mission to talk to his tenants face to face. But he wouldn't hear of that. His business could wait till the afternoon, he said. Finbar still had a few days to spare, and making nine house-calls would hardly consume as much time as that. So we set off along the motorway to Faro airport as a trio, Paul driving, me in the passenger seat with my hand resting lightly on his thigh, while Finbar sat diplomatically in the back. Then Paul stayed with me while I found a last-minute flight - and paid a premium for it. In case that isn't clear, I mean that Paul paid for it. As he'd promised he would.

I had time during the flight to Luton to decide whether to cross London and go home for the night before returning to the capital by a very early train the next morning, or to put up in central London for two nights. I quickly saw that it was a no-brainer. I had planned and prepared to be away for three whole weeks. I didn't need to return home for anything in particular: I'd get waylaid there by a pile of junk mail on the hall carpet; the house would look dirty, as it always did when I came back from a holiday, and I'd find myself pushing the vacuum-cleaner around late at night... Conscious of the obscene amount it would cost, but determined to ignore this inconvenient fact if I could, I decided I would book into a hotel in London for the two nights. And as usual, once

I'd made a decision, even one that would cost me an extravagant sum of money, I felt better at once.

While I was on the train from Luton to St Pancras I looked on my phone for a hotel. I took the cheapest offer I could find. It wasn't until I was nearly in London that I realised the place was just around the corner from the Montreal. At least it was in a part of London that I knew. I could go to my familiar Italian restaurant for my evening meal.

I texted Paul to say I'd landed safely. Hoped his day had gone OK. He texted back. All was well. We'd phone later.

A three-hour flight. But that's the net figure. Actually three-hour flights take all day. Get up early, drive to airport, check in, wait, board, taxi, fly, taxi again, disembark, walk, passports, baggage, customs, find the train station, listen to announcements with pressure-change deafened ears, take train… It was evening by the time I checked into my hotel near Marble Arch.

It was with a pleasant feeling of coming home that I went into the Montreal for a beer even though, as I looked about me, I realised there was no-one here that I knew. I "supped up", as Graham used to say, and crossed the road to my Italian place, where they were kind enough to pretend to remember me, and had spaghetti carbonara, which I find to be the most comforting of comfort dishes, provided it's cooked nicely and is not too dry.

I returned to the Montreal for a nightcap, had just the one, and tried to phone Paul. I got no answer. I wasn't terribly worried. I went back to my hotel and, feeling suddenly very tired, went straight to bed.

I was glad I hadn't gone home to Sussex when, next morning, my alarm went off at seven o'clock. It was bad enough to have to get to the Royal College of Whatever by eight thirty even when spending the night in London. Leaving from home I would have had to drive out at five o'clock.

My job for the day was to pretend to be a man with tennis elbow. Simple enough. But I had to pretend to this condition forty times during the day, with forty different examination candidates. Each of those had to diagnose the complaint, and deal with the associated issues, which were work and income related, inevitably.

If you really have tennis elbow you scream when the doctor applies certain pressures to the arm, but don't care when your arm is manipulated in other ways. You don't need to be told this: you just howl. But if you're acting it, you have to... er... act it. If you scream at the wrong moment, responding to the wrong twist-test applied by the examination candidate, the candidate will come to the wrong diagnosis and potentially fail the exam... Actually, he or she won't. The examiner will fill in an explanation card and you (or I), the role-player, will never get a day's work doing this kind of thing again.

I was careful to get everything right, minute by

minute throughout the day. With the best candidates it was easy. They knew the moves, the twist-tests, like the backs of their hands. It was the less confident candidates you had to watch. They twisted your arm this way and that, clutching at the straw that something would happen at some point that that would give them a clue... While I had to think, on the hoof, would this unfamiliar tweak make a tennis elbow patient scream in agony or not? When in doubt I would tighten my lips and grimace faintly, and look over the candidate's shoulder into the examiner's eyes for a clue as to what to do next.

My day finished at five o'clock. That was the first chance I had to phone Paul. He picked up at once. At least someone did. Actually it was Finbar. 'Oh hi,' he said.

'Oh Finbar,' I said. 'Is Paul there?'

'He is,' said Finbar, 'but he's asleep. D'you want me to wake him up?'

'Er, no,' I said. I tried to visualise the scene the other end. Had Finbar been in Paul's (and my) bedroom when the phone rang? Was he now looking down at Paul asleep on our bed? Had he – perish the thought – actually been having a siesta with Paul, in the same bed? Or had Paul left his phone in the living-room and Finbar had answered it there? I fondly hoped the last of those possible scenarios was the correct one. I said, 'Perhaps you could ask him to give me a ring when he wakes. Meanwhile, how are things?'

'Things are good,' said Finbar. He seemed to be purring like a cat down the phone. 'We got round three of the tenants already yesterday afternoon. Four more today and all was well. Just two to go tomorrow. And then...'

'And then I'll be back with you,' I said firmly. 'I phoned last night, by the way...'

'Oh,' said Finbar. 'Sorry, we had a bit of a wild evening.'

Did you indeed? I thought.

'Paul got your message but it was a bit late to call you back.'

How late did you finish, then? I wondered. 'You had a fun evening then,' I said.

'We did a few bars. Drank your health, obviously. Paul introduced me to a drink I'd never had before. Called a slippery nipple. We had about six.'

What? I thought.

'Around midnight he started asking the people behind the various bars we went to to make him banana fritters, saying he'd got a hankering for them.'

'Bloody hell,' I said. This was so unlike the Paul I knew that I had trouble getting my head round it.

'He did it in English, so I had to translate. I told them he was a total nutcase, of course. But in one bar they said yes, they'd do it, and they did. We're going back there tonight...'

'I'll be back with you tomorrow,' I said, and I heard something more steely in my voice than I'd ever heard there before. 'But about last night... You drove back?'

'No,' said Finbar. We got a taxi. Took another one back this morning to collect the car...'

I cut him off. 'Just tell him to fucking phone me.'

I ended the call. My heart was lower than my boots. Paul and Finbar had been having a whale of a time together, evidently. No, they probably hadn't had sex together, the rational side of me said. Nevertheless, they'd been having more fun without me that they'd ever had with me – and more than Paul and I together had ever had.

I took the tube back to Marble Arch. There was my hotel, or there was the Montreal. Well, I wasn't going to go to bed at six o'clock in the evening, was I? I went to the Montreal.

I looked around as I walked towards the bar but, just like last night, saw no-one there I knew. I ordered myself a pint of Guinness. Don't know why. I just felt like it. Like spaghetti carbonara it can be very comforting. I stood at the bar to drink it, watching the bar-men. One of them in particular was quite eye-catching. It gave me something to do.

A few minutes later I felt one of my buttocks being

stroked by a warm hand, while another hand came over my shoulder and deposited a half-empty beer glass on the counter next to mine. The touch on the bum was a bit of a surprise, though rather a pleasant one. I turned round and found myself looking into a pair of big brown eyes that I already knew. They belonged to Duarte.

'Oh, hi,' I said. Then, 'Good to see you.'

'It's good to see you too, Peter,' Duarte said. 'I've missed you.' He embraced me suddenly, quite intensely, and gave me a very tender kiss. I kissed him back, of course. How could I not?

'Well, I missed you too,' I said, being careful with my choice of tense. Duarte wasn't English, but he'd lived in England long enough to have a pretty subtle grasp of the language. He would pick up on the nuance. 'It was me that sent the last text, though.'

'I know,' said Duarte, and cast his eyes downward in his awkwardness, so that I saw the beautiful long dark lashes he had. 'I'm bad that way.' He half disengaged from the hug we were in and used his free hand to feel my cock and balls through my jeans.

'You're bad in every way,' I said. I couldn't help laughing a bit. I felt my cock stiffening. I could be bad in that way too. I could have, should have, removed his hand from my crotch but I didn't. 'Listen,' I said instead. 'A lot of things have happened since we last met. The main thing is, I've got a boyfriend now.' Duarte let me go rather quickly and looked around him in something like alarm.

'It's OK,' I said. 'He isn't here.' Then remembering
Duarte's nationality I added, 'He's actually in mainland
Portugal at this moment. The Algarve.'

Duarte moved towards me again and took both my
hands in his. 'I'm very happy to see you again. Angus is
away too. For a few days…'

'Angus?' As I said the name I remembered: that was
his elderly boyfriend's name.

'We could spend the night at Highgate together. In a
comfortable double bed, like yours…'

I squirmed. 'The thing is,' I said, 'that Paul and I are
exclusive,' At least I hoped we were. Uncomfortable
memories of my recent phone conversation with Finbar
came flooding into my mind. If the two of them *were*
actually hitting the sack together in my absence from the
Algarve, then it would be OK to take up Duarte's offer. I
remembered the lovely feel of him naked, and how
tactile he was in bed, and how he had projected his
spunk so amazingly into my wood-burning stove as he
stood wanking his beautiful cock, naked in the
firelight… I said, 'Your offer's very tempting, Duarte,
but I'm on a promise. Paul's staying with a very
handsome friend of ours in the Algarve. Just the two of
them in the house together till I get back there tomorrow.
I'm trusting the two of them to behave, and so…'

Duarte looked a bit crestfallen, but only for a moment.
His face lit up a bit shyly after he'd thought for a second

or two. 'They've got the downstairs open. We could go down there and sit on the sofa together. You know. Just a bit of a cuddle. Your boyfriend couldn't object to that.'

'Well, he could,' I said. 'And probably would.' *He would if he knew* was what I meant. The prospect of a cuddle on a sofa with Duarte had enormous appeal at that moment. I raised one knee and angled the foot that was now airborne so that I could caress the back of Duarte's calf muscle with the toe. Duarte purred and leaned into me again, arms round my back, his head on my shoulder, his cheek against mine. The smell of his skin...

It would be OK, I thought, if we simply cuddled. We wouldn't get each other's cocks out in the public space downstairs. I cast my mind back to what we'd done last time we'd been down there, three months ago. We'd got our hands inside each other's flies and held each other's cocks there in the warm darkness of our trousers; we'd felt them grow slippery with wet...

'No,' I said suddenly, pulling myself half away from him, though gently. 'I can't. We mustn't. Tell you what. I'll buy you dinner instead. Take you to the Italian place we went to before.'

Duarte's face fell. 'It's not the same,' he said.

'No,' I said, 'but it'll have to do. Have anything you like off the menu. I'll pay, like I said. And wine too.'

Duarte acknowledged defeat. 'OK, then,' he said. 'Dinner it is.' We finished our drinks and turned towards the door. As we approached it, who should come through it but Amos, my Caribbean interior designer guy with the great cock and an even greater talent for giving a blow-job. He stopped when he saw us. 'Well, if it isn't Peter,' he said. Diplomatically, since he could see I was with someone, instead of embracing me he merely shook my hand. Then he turned to Duarte, whom he'd seen and commented on once before, and made a big pantomime show of looking him up and down. Then he turned back to me. 'Well, well, well,' he said. 'Aren't you the lucky one?'

SEVENTEEN

We had rib-eye steak, after a shared platter of antipasti, and then the inevitable tiramisu. And a bottle of Sicilian merlot. After I'd paid the bill Duarte suggested we went back to the Montreal for a nightcap. I said no, I had to be up in the morning to catch a flight to Portugal. Duarte then made big eyes at me and said, then why didn't we have a nightcap together at the bar in my hotel? We certainly weren't going to do that. I'd never get him out of the place if we went to my hotel together – and I'd be hard put to it to resist the temptation he presented once he was within spitting distance of my bedroom. I said, 'And someone else has to get into the driving seat of a bus at six o'clock,' and gave him a schoolmasterly frown. To my surprise he accepted that and, after a rather heavy kiss, turned and disappeared into the night, waving back at me from the corner with Oxford Street before he turned towards the tube station.

I went back to my hotel alone, and had a single brandy in the nearly empty bar. While I was drinking it Paul phoned me and we had a longish chat, during which we both managed to avoid mentioning Finbar. I was glad of that. I did tell him, though, that I'd bumped into Duarte and we'd had dinner together. Paul seemed OK with that and we both left it there. In fact, when we ended the call on the usual antiphonal diminuendo of good-nights and I-love-yous, I felt buoyed by the positive mood of our phone-call. I went up to my room, to my bed, and got into it, then had a fairly major wank, not bothering to mop up afterwards but, heedless of what the chambermaids might say in the morning, leaving things to dry naturally while I slept. I felt I owed myself that solitary pleasure after my heroic refusal to give in to the temptations presented by my Madeiran friend. I rather hoped that Paul would now be enjoying himself in the same manner, celebrating, as I was, the happy spirit of that last phone-call. Enjoying himself – at least I hoped this would be the case – without the bedtime company of Finbar.

Among the satisfactory things I'd learnt from Paul in the course of his call to me was that he and Finbar had completed the nine face-to-face meetings with the Algarve tenants. They were all satisfied as to his identity, and all apologised for having been tricked into handing the previous instalment of their rent to someone else. Though that was hardly their fault: a good con-man is a good con-man. There was no sign yet of Paul's money coming back to him; perhaps it never would. At least his prompt action had staunched the haemorrhage.

Another thing I was, in a way, pleased with was that Finbar would be flying back to London a few hours after Paul met me at Faro. It was agreed that the three of us would have lunch together somewhere in Faro, then return to the airport to drop Finbar off. I was able to mull over all this good news on the train out to Luton, also on the flight across Biscay, Spain and Portugal. It was good to have something to think about. I didn't have a window seat this time, but sat next to a woman with a baby that had ear-ache the whole way and wanted to share the bad news.

Finbar looked lovely when I saw him in the arrivals hall. Still in his shorts, looking relaxed and slightly tanned after his stay. Paul, a bit more stork-like in his own shorts than Finbar, looked lovely too. They made a handsome pair. The best thing about the way they looked together was the obvious fact that they hadn't had sex or shared a bed while I'd been away. How did I know this? Because if they had done I would have seen it in their eyes and in their demeanour. You always do.

We drove to a sea-front restaurant on the main promenade in Faro. We sat out in the sun and watched the planes coasting down across the lagoon towards the airport, flashing as they caught the midday sun. 'You had a good evening again last night?' I said to Finbar.

'Very good,' he said. 'But we didn't need a taxi back home. The car knew the way by now. Neither of us exactly drove.'

I let that go. 'But no banana fritters, I suppose,' I suggested.

'Oh, we had those again,' said Finbar, deadpan. An hour later we drove him back to the airport and saw him through the departure gate.

'Sad to see him go,' I admitted to Paul.

'Yeah, but we'll be seeing him again in a week or so. You're lucky to have such a good friend.' I remembered that he'd said that before.

Paul and I spent what remained of the afternoon lounging about our garden and skinny-dipping in the pool. We'd decided to stay on out here a couple more days before using the second part of our open-ended return tickets back to Rome.

We had a go at something else during the afternoon, in the bedroom, but it didn't quite work so we gave it up for the time being. The business of love is an ongoing negotiation, and Paul and I had a luxury that not all negotiators have: we had all the time in the world; we could "come back to it later" whenever we wanted to.

When it got to be time to go out and eat and drink something I asked Paul where he wanted to go. Perhaps to the place he'd had the banana fritters twice with Finbar? I'd be quite happy if he wanted to do that again.

'That was a place in Albufeira,' Paul said. 'I don't specially want to go back to it tonight. I want to take you somewhere else.'

He drove me through the dusk to a restaurant in the middle of nowhere, halfway to Armaçao de Pera, where we parked the car on such an incline outside that we carefully wedged a stone under one wheel just in case. The restaurant was very small; the meal was cosy and intimate. It was like a foretaste of dining in our own dining-room – if and when the day should come when we would share one – but with the advantage that neither of us would have to think about doing the washing-up afterwards.

As we waited for our fresh prawn starter Paul said, 'I suppose I should explain what happened between me and Finbar.'

'You don't have to,' I said. 'I mean, feel free, but there's nothing you need to say. I know you haven't had sex together. I'm glad about that. I also know you've grown very fond of him, and I don't have a problem there.'

Paul didn't give me one of his lopsided grins just then. He looked me full in the face, wearing astonishment on his. 'How do you know we haven't slept together? I thought I'd be having to convince you... How can you tell?'

'Because I'm three years older than you are...' I couldn't keep a straight face. I broke into a grin and so did he. I went on, 'No, seriously, I'd have seen it in your eyes if you had. And you haven't. I know. Listen, I saw Duarte last night, as you know. It was quite by chance. He actually invited me back to his boyfriend's house in Highgate because Angus, the boyfriend, was away. It was tempting but I said no. We did have dinner together; we hugged and kissed a couple of times, and I hope that's OK with you, but that was all.' It hadn't quite been all, but it was almost all, and I thought I'd probably said as much as I needed to.

Paul looked slightly uncomfortable for a moment. Then he said, 'Well, if we're being totally honest, I did have a goodnight hug with Finbar too.' He shrugged his shoulders. 'And yes, it was very nice, I have to say.'

'Fair enough,' I said. 'Was that last night or the one before?'

I didn't realise how wicked this question was until Paul answered it. 'Both,' he said, a bit sheepishly.

'I can't complain,' I said. 'I've hugged Finbar too. Though only once before this last week. It was when Portia was killed. Before I drove round to your place and threw myself at you... I know Finbar's very physically attractive, as well as being a lovely guy.'

'Yes,' said Paul, visibly relieved. 'He is attractive. Sometimes even two straight guys notice that about each other...'

'I understand,' I said. Then, 'I suppose, if we're all being scrupulously honest I have to tell you that Duarte did grab my cock through my trousers. When we were in the Montreal.'

'Did you grab his?' Paul not unnaturally wanted to know.

'Actually no,' I said. 'But I didn't push his hand away. Sorry, but I did let him have a bit of a feel.'

'It's OK,' said Paul, though a bit unsteadily. 'Were you stiff? How do you like the prawns, by the way?'

'Half-hard, I suppose,' I admitted. 'And I'm loving the prawns.'

'Good,' said Paul. 'And actually, something a bit surprising happened last night.' *Oh yeah?* 'When Finbar and I were saying goodnight, his hand accidentally found its way round my cock.'

It must have been quite a goodnight hug, I thought. I said, 'Oh yeah?'

'But having found it, his fingers clasped it quite attentively, if that's the right word.'

'Conveys the meaning perfectly.'

'I mean, only for a second or two,' Paul said hastily. 'But – and it must be something to do with me discovering I'm a bit gay, through you – I found my reflex was to grab his too.'

'Oh wow,' I said. 'Um – I mean, actually… how big is he?' I was appalled but thrilled. I'd secretly wanted a feel of Finbar's cock for years. How had Paul got there before me?

'Same size as me,' Paul said.

'I'd kind of guessed.' And now – well, I had to ask, 'Was he stiff? Were you?'

Paul puffed out his cheeks and exhaled. 'How stiff is stiff? No, not really. OK… Still pointing down, not up, in both cases, but halfway there.'

'Wow,' I said, a bit unsteadily.

'But that was the end of it,' Paul said rather intensely.

'We gave each other a goodnight peck on the cheek and went to our separate rooms.'

I said, 'And this happened...?'

'Just after my phone-call with you.'

Just after? I thought. Just after that intimate and loving conversation with me you were groping and kissing Finbar?! A cold wind of anger and shock blew through me. And then it blew away. What did it matter if my two best friends had kissed each other, and whether that had happened before or after a phone-call with me? Paul and I loved each other. We'd worn our hearts on our sleeves together, and with other friends – friends we'd hugged and kissed as recently as twenty hours ago. Paul hadn't gone to bed with Finbar, in any of the senses in which that Tardis-like expression can be used, and I hadn't gone to bed with Duarte. The latter fact I knew. The former I just had to believe. But I did believe Paul. And I will do to my dying day.

'And after that I went to bed and had a wank,' said Paul, startling me.

When I'd recovered, 'I'm not surprised,' I said. I chuckled. 'Me too.'

When it came to bedtime that night everything went very nicely indeed. And so did 'everything' in the days that followed, as we relaxed and got back into holiday mood at Paul's Portuguese hideaway, before returning like homing swallows to Rome.

There, we explored the sights. We made a point of kissing each other very publicly at each of the hallowed landmarks we visited: Forum, Pantheon, Coliseum, and even right next to Bernini's Baldacchino canopy over the high altar in St Peter's. Was such a kiss as that last one sacrilegious? we asked ourselves. We came to an unshakeably firm answer. That not only do bride and bridegroom kiss before the high altar at the crux of the marriage rite, but that the expression of true love can not be a sacrilege anywhere.

I found myself asking myself another question as we explored the wonders of the city. It was about the nature of the attraction between Finbar and Paul. I didn't find any words, though, in which I could broach the question – and assuage my curiosity – with Paul. Not yet, at least. But I had easier things to ponder. If Paul and I could kiss so easily in St Peter's, with the witness of all the world, would we be able to do the same when we returned to East Sussex? In the King Billy? In the Harrow? In the streets of Rye? This was easy only in that it was easy to formulate the question. The answer still eluded me and I guessed that it more than eluded Paul.

And then another question posed itself. We had kissed under the dome of St Peter's church in Rome. Would we ever tie the knot officially? Get married to each other in other words, as in English law we were now allowed to do?

I parked that last question for now, while the one

about the King Billy and the Harrow would answer itself in another week or so when we next might find ourselves inside those hallowed walls. In the meantime we said goodbye after a few days to the hectic splendour of Rome and drove south to the more relaxing town of Sorrento.

We stayed in a cliff-top hotel where Henrik Ibsen had stayed: he had written part of his chilly play 'Ghosts' here. The sea-view windows gave onto a spectacle that was far from chilly, even if there must be ghosts enough out there. For here within the window's frame lay the city of Naples directly ahead, nine miles across the bay that shares the city's name. To the east of the city, to the right, stood Vesuvius, its head intermittently among the clouds. Invisible at the mountain's foot were buried Herculaneum and Pompeii. And, looking leftward from the Naples sprawl, there in the western sea lay the island of Ischia, black on silver in the morning sun, while tantalisingly out of sight, hidden by the headland on which our hotel perched, was the island of Capri.

We visited some of those places by boat in the course of our stay. And then one night, as we sat in the trattoria that had become our favourite eating place during our stay, I found the words to ask Paul what I'd wanted to. They were simple enough after all. 'Tell me,' I said to him, 'what it is with Finbar and you?'

Paul grinned across the table at me, and not at all lopsidedly. 'I've been waiting for you to ask that for days,' he said. 'Spent a lot of time turning over possible answers in my mind.' He reached for the bottle of red wine that stood between us on the table and topped both our glasses up. 'Thing is, when you grow up straight, or thinking you're straight, or wanting to be straight, in your teens, you still find yourself drawn to some people of your own sex – your teen best mates... Sometimes there's a more emotional bond.'

'Same thing here,' I said deadpan. 'Everyone grows up wanting to be straight. I certainly did.'

'And most people who're mainly straight...' He paused. Then, thoughtfully, 'Do I include myself these days? I'm not sure... Perhaps that's a question for another day... Anyway, they find that thoughts of women, fantasies about women, lusting after women, then acting on that... it all begins to take over so strongly that the other is pushed to one side, then squashed completely, and as the years pass, almost forgotten about.'

'I realise that,' I said. 'I understand. I used to think that would happen with me. But the years passed and it never did. Perhaps because my feelings for other boys grew in me so early – because my experiences with boys began so early – they stayed strong. I never found a friendship with a woman, or a fantasy about a woman even, that was strong enough to push them out of the way.'

'Hold that thought for later,' Paul said. 'I do want to hear about all that. Your early stuff, I mean. But it'll have to be another time, or we'll get all tangled up and I'll forget what I was trying to say.'

'We should have written an agenda on a piece of paper,' I said with a straight face. Paul smiled.

'What happened after I met you,' he went on, 'was that I had to question everything. It was easier for you. You'd lived with a man for years. I guess you'd been in love with other men before, and I know you've had sex with other men because you've told me so. But for me... I was like a caterpillar that becomes a chrysalis and everything gets liquefied inside before it's reassembled into the cells that will become a butterfly.' He took my hand across the table. 'I'm still going through this process. You'll need to understand that and be patient with me.'

I couldn't get any words out. I gave his hand a squeeze.

'Part of the process has been remembering those things in the past, those gay memories I'd almost deleted from my memory bank, and bringing them back to life. Getting a bit drunk with you and Finbar made me think about them. Then, as you know, in the wake of Finbar's surprising revelations – and your unexpected adventure on Praia Grande – I found myself blurting them out. OK, I'd already noticed Finbar was attractive when I first saw him and sat beside him in your car when, weirdly, he was driving it. I felt – cliché coming here – like we were kindred spirits, soul-mates who hadn't yet met. And especially because he was a friend of yours, I wanted to find out more.'

'And you got the chance,' I said. 'Because he happens

to speak – because I happened to mention that he speaks – Portuguese. I had found myself wishing – and this is a dreadful admission of jealousy, and it doesn't reflect well on me – that you'd had your problems in Almería, and I could have used my Spanish to help you sort them out, without involving Finbar.'

'I know you wished that,' said Paul softly. 'I could see it. I understand.' He took a gulp of wine and I copied him. 'I was right in a way. Finbar is a straight guy with gay things buried in the strata of his experience. My hunch was correct. But I wanted to explore him a bit further. And here I owe an apology to you. I shouldn't even have wanted that.'

'It's OK, Paul,' I said. 'It's all OK.'

'Even though we got no further than a couple of drunken evenings in your absence which were a bit soul-baring, and a kiss and a grope which I've already told you about.'

'It's all OK,' I said. I could sense, though there was no visible sign of it, that Paul was welling up inside, and that had the effect of making the same thing happen inside me. We were still squeezing hands across the table-top for all the world to witness.

I said, 'We understand each other. Everything between us is fine. And it'll be fine with us and Finbar when we're back home. You'll see.'

I poured us another glass of wine. Perhaps we really would need a written agenda next time we had discussions of this sort. In which case, I thought, under *Any Other Business* could come some sharing with me – by Paul – of the soul-baring conversations between Finbar and him on those drunken evenings when I wasn't there…

EIGHTEEN

On our last day in Sorrento we drove round the headland and explored the chain of villages that form the Amalfi Coast. The sea road plunged up and down among pine-clad rocky hills and corkscrewed round gnarled outcrops, and the sea, now that we looked south and sunward across it, was a beast of a very different colour – lavender and diamond-flashing – from the cobalt-enamelled one that, facing north, we saw from our hotel.

We came back tired with the concentration of the vertiginous drive (Paul and I had taken the wheel in turns) and ended up proud of our adventurous spirits but relieved to be home, in our favourite trattoria once again. We had an aperitiferous prosecco (no, don't check: I made the adjective up myself) and ordered pasta, with a veal escalope to follow. 'So tonight,' said Paul, as we clinked glasses, 'which bit of the agenda shall we do?'

'We could do the item headed, How Peter Found Out That He Was Gay. Since I've been promising it for what seems like an age.'

'Pity Finbar's not still around,' said Paul. 'I think he was rather looking forward to that too.'

'I'm sure he was,' I said. 'Perhaps we can reprise it by popular demand when we're back at home.' I was joking, or thought I was. Yet as I said the words I found myself thinking fondly about how nice that would be. The three of us back together again and talking about sex again. What a difference a week makes.

'Well, anyway, here goes.' I launched in. 'Like I said, there was never a girl or woman in my life who made enough impression on me sexually to supersede the impression already made by boys. The first of those impressions I remember clearly was one made by a boy called James. We went to the beach at Camber Sands with our two pairs of parents and went off and played in the dunes.'

'Shades of Praia Grande?' Paul said with a bit of a smirk.

'You have to start somewhere,' I replied. 'We were excavating dry sand and piling it up in heaps, just for the fun of it. Then without any sign of inhibition, and without turning even partly aside, James, who was kneeling in the sand, pulled his cock out over the top of his swimming trunks and pissed, facing me just a foot away, smiling into my eyes.

'I smiled back at him and instinctively copied his action in every detail. We ended up crossing swords – the first time I'd done that in my life, and of course I'd no idea that was what it was called. When we'd finished we should have tucked our dicks away but we didn't. Instead we gave each other a naughty look, and giggled, and then spontaneously we reached out for each other's and touched and fingered them, and felt what little there was to feel of each other's olive-sized balls. We were daintily erect by then, but a moment later a chill of fear came down on us: an awareness that we were doing

Anthony McDonald

something that we weren't supposed to do. Perhaps that's another way of saying we knew we'd have been severely told off if we'd got caught.

'We did tuck ourselves away then. I remember James's stayed semi-rigid a little longer inside his trunks than mine did. I remember how much I loved that sight. But that was the end of it. James wasn't a neighbour, his grandparents were neighbours, and he was on a visit from miles away. I'm not sure I ever saw him again.

'But the memory lingered, and so did my desire for James. It strengthened, didn't weaken as time passed. My desire for James. Or at least someone very like James. For that I had to wait four years.'

'Which makes you eleven at the time,' said Paul.

'We both were. The other boy and I. Who was called Alan. We met when we started secondary school together. We kind of fell for each other at first meeting. Showing off our best pen-knives. I think I saw a reincarnation of James in him. And – how do I know?, but I've sometimes wondered – perhaps he saw a reincarnation of somebody else in me.

'We were best friends for about two years. We never did anything together, in the the way of playing with cocks, I mean. We only ever saw each other's by chance occasionally, standing next to each other at the urinals. I remember that his looked just like mine...'

'Pretty big, then, for an eleven-year-old's,' said Paul, deadpan.

'I meant, like mine did at that age. Obviously... I liked the look of it. In a narcissistic way perhaps. Daintily tapering and tasselled it was...'

'As yours still is, my darling.'

'Thank you.' I made a mock-bow across the table in acknowledgement of the jokey compliment. 'It was friendship, but of a special kind. I felt something quite different for Alan, something I didn't feel for my other friends at all.'

'It was love,' Paul said, and I saw in his eyes that he was serious now.

I nodded. 'Thank you. Yes, looking back now, I think it might have been. Whatever it was, no girl could ever get to me in the way that Alan did. Can't explain it. It's just the way it was.'

'What happened to Alan?'

'A couple of years later he moved away. I've no idea if he turned out gay. No idea whether, if he'd stayed and we'd gone through puberty together, we might have got things together in a sexual way.'

'Ah,' said Paul. 'Maybe it was best the way it was. Love un-tasted being the sweetest love of all.'

'Point taken,' I said. 'But you're the sweetest love of all, and you're hardly un-tasted. I mean, you're hardly un-tasted by me.' I might have been bantering, but the nub of what I said was true. Knowing, loving, having,

Paul, and belonging to Paul, were the sweetest experiences I knew. What?! Sweeter than those twenty years of loving Graham and being loved by him? Uncomfortable thought. But I couldn't compare the two. Love merges. Great love past and great love present surrender their separate identities and become one. Arithmetical ideas of comparison and scale fade and become meaningless things. There was no *greater than*, no *less than*, in the cases of dead Graham and quick Paul. In loving Paul totally there lay no disrespect to Graham's memory.

I had to jolt myself out of a train of thought that was, in its way, impossibly private, and continue the narrative I was relating to Paul. 'Yes,' I said. 'I think it was love. A first tentative flowering, like a snowdrop in February. But then he left and three years went by.'

'And...?'

'And I had my first taste of sex with another boy. My first taste of sex with anyone else at all. And if we agreed the other day that there was no sacrilege in our kissing by the high altar of St Peter's in Rome, well, what happened to me – what I did, since I wasn't raped and it takes two to tango...'

'Just go on,' said Paul.

'I sang in the choir at school. I was an alto till my voice broke. Then there was an interval of six months or so while I couldn't sing at all. Then I came back to the choir, reincarnated as a tenor. We had a chapel and in the chapel was an organ loft. We, the choir, sat on benches around the organ. The choir leader, who was also a tenor, was about a year older than me. He was very masculine and handsome: things I couldn't help noticing. I was acquiring a taste in men's appearances. Michael Saddler was his name. After we'd had a practice it was Michael's job to put the music away and tidy up. Because I liked him...'

'Because you fancied him...'

I let that go. 'I used to stay and help him sometimes. One evening we'd just finished tidying the books away when he suddenly sat down on the organist's bench-seat with his back to the console. He'd never done that before, at least, not with me. I looked at him, slightly puzzled. 'Pete,' he said, and he'd never called me Pete before either, "Want to sit with me?"

'"Sit next to you?" I asked, not catching on, though I did notice that he didn't pat the bench beside him the way people who're making that invitation usually do.

'He gave me a curious look that I'd never seen him give me before. "On top of me." In a businesslike manner he smacked the tops of both his thighs. I thought this was funny and I laughed. But I took his invitation up. I was intrigued. I didn't know what he was playing at. But of course a part of me certainly did.'

'Your cock, I suppose,' said Paul.

'I didn't mean that,' I said, 'but yes, that too. Of course, as soon as I sat across his knees his hand found my erection easily and gave it a squeeze. He asked me if I'd still stay sitting there if he had his trousers down and if he took mine down too. I said, yes, probably, and a moment later we both had our uniform trousers down to the knees. His just above. Mine – he saw to it – just below. I later realised why. I just had time to glimpse his standing dick and to see that it was an unthreatening half-size smaller than my own, before I sat back down on his lap. I knew by then what he wanted to do and, more surprisingly, that it was what I wanted too. I angled myself as well as I could towards his dick and, with a bit of a wriggle, he impaled me on it. It went in surprisingly easily.'

'To the manner born, you.'

'He told me I needed to bounce up and down a bit, and I obliged. He was good enough to try and wank me a bit while I rode him, but his heart wasn't really in it. He abandoned that as soon as he felt himself start to come – it took less than half a minute anyway – and when he'd finished his climax I climbed off him a bit shakily. I pulled my trousers back up and he did his too, very quickly. It wasn't till then that I realised I'd been fucked *in chapel* of all places. Well,' I stopped and took a slug of wine. 'That was the story of my first time.'

'Maybe that had better be enough for now,' said Paul, fidgeting his long legs under the table. 'Otherwise I'll find myself coming at dinner in a restaurant. And that would be a first for me.'

'Don't you want to hear how I finished myself off?' I

asked naughtily.

'Well, all right, though I could probably guess. You completed the wank when you got home.'

'Before then,' I said. 'When I got to the bus stop there was no-one there. I stood inside the shelter, facing into the corner, tightly wedging myself in there, and put one hand into my pocket, and came inside my trousers after a moment or two. What happened when I got home was I realised I needed to do something I hadn't thought about. I.e. dash to the loo and empty my backside.'

'Ah,' said Paul. 'What goes up must come down. But better stop there. The waiter's just arriving with our taglioline now.'

We had come on holiday planning not to drive long distances. But without thinking about it we'd boxed ourselves into a corner. In three hops we'd drifted four hundred miles south from our arrival airport of Pisa. We decided we'd divide the journey back into two, staying one night at Viterbo, just north of Rome, on our way. It was another town that nestled in a fairly complete set of medieval walls, another town that had been a papal residence in times of trouble centuries ago. It had its papal palace and its handsome square. We had a pleasant walk around the town when we arrived in the late afternoon, but were beginning to feel that three weeks was about long enough to have been away. In the morning we set off early for Pisa, and boarded our homebound plane.

It was a journey on rewind. The flight to Gatwick. The slow train to Hastings. Finbar waiting outside the station at the wheel of my Jaguar that had once been his, ready to drive us home. So much had happened to all of us since he had driven us to this station just three weeks ago. So much had happened between the three of us, Paul, Finbar and me, that it felt, travelling that short road home, as though we were three different men from the three who had so recently travelled it together going the other way. But the thing that surprised me most was the unexpected happiness that rose in me at my first sight of Finbar, getting out of my car to welcome us back, and the evident delight with which he greeted not just Paul but also me.

'So what's next for you two?' Finbar asked us brightly – I sat next to him while Paul was in the back this time round – without taking his eyes off the road.

'Meaning?' asked Paul.

'Moving in together? Emigrating to Portugal?'

Did Finbar know that those were the two things I was dreaming about, silly as a lovesick schoolgirl, but hadn't yet approached within a million miles of bringing up with Paul?

Not giving Paul a chance to answer I said, 'As far as I'm concerned Paul can move in with me tomorrow. I only need to make a bit of space in the wardrobe. It just isn't so easy for Paul.'

'And why would that be?' Finbar asked, apparently innocently.

I still didn't let Paul get a word in. 'He doesn't think the judgemental worlds of Rye and Icklesham are ready for him to come out as gay. He'll have enough trouble walking into the King Billy or the Harrow with me as it is. I think the chances of us moving in together in any foreseeable future are pretty slim.'

'The world of Albufeira and Faro seemed to have no trouble with you both,' said Finbar reasonably. 'Even I thought you were both a bit on the cheeky side out there.'

'The difference,' intervened Paul, 'is that nobody knows me in Albufeira or Faro. Unlike in Rye. We even kissed beside the high altar in St Peter's in Rome, and that was OK because nobody knew us there either.'

Finbar ignored the last bit. 'Nobody knows me,' you say. 'Hey, Paul, shouldn't I be hearing a bit of an *us* and *we?*'

'Apologies all round,' said Paul a bit huffily, 'if I've offended anyone…'

Finbar cut him off. 'I thought you might be hungry when you got back, and have nothing in.' Then more diffidently he went on, 'I've done a bit of a stew. Enough to share if you both wanted to. Be nice to have some company…'

I jumped in before Paul had a chance to say no. I felt

myself getting oddly upset at the thought of Finbar dining alone with a huge pot of stew that, if we didn't take up his offer, would go on for days. 'That'd be lovely, Finbar. I'll accept, even if Paul won't. It's very kind of you.'

Finbar's tone resumed its usual carefree confidence. 'Well, if Paul does decide to join us, he might like to know I've gone on the internet and looked up a recipe.'

'A recipe for what?' came Paul's voice from the back seat.

'Do you need to ask?' said Finbar in a very serious tone. 'Banana fritters, obviously.'

NINETEEN

The stew was great and so were the fritters, and the evening was more than convivial. When the three of us said goodnight there were parting hugs all round, and kisses on the lips, no less. I was tempted to grab Finbar's cock through his trousers, and perhaps the same thought occurred to everyone, but we all (I'm guessing) decided prudently that that might have been going too far and could have unleashed who knew what genies from bottles that it would be safer not to know about.

Paul didn't go home that night. He walked with me the few paces from Finbar's house to mine – where I'd had the forethought to put the heating on before going into Finbar's for our meal. I couldn't help wishing, as we walked, that Finbar could be coming back with us too, and tried to imagine, yet tried not to at the same time, a future in which the three of all lived together under the same roof and shared the same bed. I wondered if, one day when I was drunk enough, I'd find myself putting this to Paul.

Paul drove off at first light as usual. That had been one thing back in March's dark mornings, when we'd first met. Now, in late May, it meant a four in the morning wake-up. But we both had work to catch up on after three weeks away, and four thirty didn't seem, in the circumstances, too early to start. An hour later I heard Finbar's car (he had a newer, better Jaguar now) leave his driveway three doors away and head off to wherever he was going to insert his hand – the one he'd stroked my hair with as recently as during last night's parting kiss – into the innards of a horse or cow.

I had some writing to catch up on: a couple of deadlines to not miss. I phoned the King Billy to check my shifts. They wouldn't need me behind the bar for a couple more days. I wasn't too sorry. I had returned to a big backlog of writing tasks. I rolled up my sleeves, quite literally, and got on with them.

Soon after midday Finbar phoned. What about the three of us, Finbar, Paul and me, meeting up in the King Billy for a drink this evening, then going on somewhere for a meal? This flustered me. It seemed that Finbar wanted to keep on going with the thing, whatever it was, that we had all got a buzz out of in Portugal. Being the three of us. The brain works quickly. Yes, I wanted the three of us. I also wanted Paul all to myself. The tongue lags behind a little way. I said, 'Do we need three cars?'

We made the logical arrangement. Paul, who lived the furthest from the King Billy of all of us, would drive to where Finbar and I lived nearly next door to each other, pick us up and drive us all to the pub. How we all returned home, and to which one or ones, could be negotiated later.

Later, waiting for Paul to come and pick us up, I took a shower, then spent some time in front of the mirror, working out what I would wear. Did I just write that? I, confident and self-assured at the age of fifty plus, with most of my life's experience of going on dates with people of whatever sex well behind me, stood in front of a mirror, breathing my tummy in, and wishing it even a bit further in than that, and trying on shirts and jeans because I was going to a pub with two male friends.

Back in Portugal, ten days ago, I'd given no thought to this. We'd been three guys, acting like more-or-less straight guys, thrown together by circumstances, dealing with a crisis in the life of one of us, and had simply chucked on the clothes we felt were right for going to a police station, for instance, and in the evenings, well, we hadn't really given it a thought. Although, now I did think about it, we had somehow made a point during those evenings of putting on shorts that showed our legs off to best advantage...

It was a warm evening for May. I chose a pair of pale blue jeans that were quite tight-fitting, with white socks and trainers underneath. I chose a chunky leather belt to round off the effect, and then a pastel-blue shirt with white collar and cuffs. If the others were to decide I looked a bit too gay, well they were welcome to tell me so.

Paul phoned to say he'd pick Finbar and me up in ten minutes. He was on his way. Presumably he phoned Finbar a moment before or just after, because when I went out into the road five minutes later Finbar was coming out of his house too. He was wearing a pair of tight blue jeans I'd never seen him in before. Tightly drawn in with a chestnut-shiny leather belt. White socks and trainers, and a cream shirt with broad shoulders and voluptuously wide sleeves. He took my breath away. I'd never seen him dressed anything like this before. I'd never seen him looking lovelier than he did now.

Women say things to each other like, "Love that necklace / broach / skirt." Blokes don't. Finbar and I stood together at the roadside pretending we hadn't noticed how we were dressed. We shared a few mundane details of the day we'd each separately had, and then Paul's planet blue Kia Ceed hove into view quite fast…

The etiquette is older than the invention of motor cars. The acknowledged lovers sit together in the front; the third party, whatever his or her long-term game may be, sits in the back. So it was with us on that two-mile drive to the King Billy. From my ringside seat, therefore, I was able to notice that Paul too was dressed in tight-fitting pale blue jeans, white socks and trainers. His shirt, which was white with thin blue stripes, suited him well and looked lovely. OK, it would have looked lovely to anyone. In my eyes it looked gorgeous. It also looked as though he'd bought it in the eighties when that type of striped shirt was fashionable, and had kept it ever since. Just in case the moment should ever come… OK, the moment had come. Tonight. Most certainly it had. I wasn't going to tell him this, though. Well, not right now.

Dressed as we were, the three of us walking into the King Billy together created a bit of a *phrvfthphrvrph*. I can't find any other way to render the mutter that arose from the knot of regulars as we arrived.

Hannah was behind the bar. I lifted the drawbridge as soon as I saw her and walked into the hallowed space where, when I was on duty, I would work among the pumps and shelves of glasses, and gave her a kiss. A second before our embrace I saw that things were not right. 'Mmmm?' I asked.

She beckoned with her eyes and we walked quickly into the quiet and private space between the bar and kitchen where, between staff members at the King Billy, all confidences were shared. Hannah said, 'We've split up. Dave and me.'

'Of course Dave and you,' I said. 'You wouldn't be splitting up with anyone else.' I paused. 'Unless, like Rip Van Winkle, I'd been away for longer than I imagined. But – sorry – I'm being flippant and you're serious…' I gave her another kiss. 'Er… I'm here with two friends. I'd better get back to them. Catch up soon…'

The evening grew lovely. One pint became two, became three. We didn't go elsewhere to eat. We sat down, the three of us, and shared a pint of prawns, and had hake and chips. We didn't have room for pudding but had one anyway. Don't know why, but I never remember what I had for pudding. It wasn't banana fritters. Finbar and I squashed Paul firmly when he wanted to order that. As a part-time employee of the place I'd never have lived it down.

Paul drove us back to my place, which was the nearest one. His driving was a bit alarming. 'You're on the wrong side of the road,' I said to him in a whispered yell of terror at one point, and I heard my gasp echoed by Finbar in the back. 'I know,' Paul said. 'I'd dropped something on the floor and was looking for it.'

Tout comprendre, c'est tout pardonner. To understand all is to forgive all. As Evelyn Waugh had Sebastian say when he puked in through Charles's Oxford college window. But there are exceptions. I wrenched the wheel away from Paul and we successfully anchored in my driveway. But it took me nearly forty seconds to forgive him…

There was a murmur of *my place or his, or his.* We all went to mine. There would be no question of Paul driving home now, and Finbar only had thirty yards to walk to his, so I didn't have qualms about finding us a nightcap. It was sloe gin that I'd made the year before and of which just a little remained, survivor of the ravages of last Christmas.

'Well, you've done it,' Finbar said. A bit smugly. 'Walked into the King Billy together as a couple.' What he meant was that *he* had done it. Which, to be fair to him, he had.

'We went in like a threesome,' Paul said, a little less happily. 'Don't know how that's going to go down.'

'For God's sake, it doesn't matter,' I said, feeling momentarily exasperated with him. 'None of those people in the King Billy are your clients or tenants. What they say can't hurt you. You're six foot one and built of steel. Nobody's going to beat you up.'

Paul looked at me. 'I was thinking of you,' he said, and wrung my heart.

'The Plough next,' said Finbar brightly, wisely ignoring that last exchange.

'Yes,' I said. I looked at him. He looked even lovelier after an evening's drinking than he had before it began. It occurred to me that it might not be the Plough next, but bed next – for all three of us. My bed was a very wide one and none of us were outsize, Paul and I being very slim and Finbar only marginally stockier...

But a few minutes later Finbar broke the spell. 'Right,' he said. 'Time I left you to it and took myself to bed.' He got to his feet a bit unsteadily. 'Definitely do the Plough in a day or two.' Then I got to my feet and so did Paul.

I said to Paul mock-sternly, 'You're not going home. You're staying with me.'

He said, 'I was going to do that anyway.' I was glad.

The three of us found our way into the hall. Finbar threw his arms round me, then embraced Paul. Then back to me. We kissed. And now it was my turn to be the bad boy. I clutched at Finbar's dick through his jeans, and found it easily. It wasn't hard but even so it hung a startlingly long way down inside his trouser-leg. I was hardly making a secret of this: my hand was in full view of Paul, standing shoulder to shoulder with me. I said, 'God, you're as big as Paul.'

'I know,' Finbar said, and then I felt his hand come exploringly against my own crotch. 'Hmmm,' he said, 'I can't find yours.' But immediately afterwards he did.

'You may be disappointed there,' I said.

'Not at all,' said Finbar, not taking his hand away but giving my thickening member a jolly good feel.

'Now, you two,' said Paul, sounding a bit uneasy. But then he dealt with his unease by groping Finbar's. Then there we were in a three-way embrace, and zips were beginning to go down.

It was Finbar who came to his senses first. 'OK, guys, we'd better stop now. Or we'll regret things in the morning.'

It took us a few more seconds to pull away from one another but we somehow managed it. We opened the front door and let in the cold night air, which sobered us a bit. There were a couple of final kisses in the doorway, then Paul and I let Finbar walk out and get on his way. We watched him go. He disappeared for a second beyond the throw of our outside light, and then his own light came on automatically as he approached his door, and he turned and gave us a wave like a pantomime character who appears with a flash of light on stage. The effect was striking – and appropriate. Paul and I shut our own front door and went inside.

I had time over the next few days to reflect on what I just wrote there. The throw of *our* outside light. We shut *our own* front door...

I had time enough for thinking. I suddenly got a few days' role-play work in London, where an actor colleague was kind enough to put me up on his sofa for the nights in between. At the same time Paul got called down to Cornwall to sort a few things out with tenants there. Nothing major. He didn't need my support, and he didn't need translation into Portuguese. He got my phone-calls, of course, and texts and emails, and I got his. I even exchanged a few emails with Finbar.

So, *our* outside light, *our own* front door. If our 'coming-out', at a combined age of ninety-nine, inside the august precincts of the Harrow was to be our next step into the unknown, then the business of moving in together might be the one that followed that. Paul and I hadn't really discussed this yet. We'd made jokes about it and said, wouldn't it be nice, but that was as far as we'd got. But I thought long and hard about it now. Moving in together at twenty is already a big deal. At fifty... Well, it would be far from straightforward. There was his place and there was mine. His was more modern, better appointed, cheaper to heat and easier to clean and run.

Yet I had a problem on my side already. It sounds silly, but I really didn't want to move away from Finbar. It wasn't just that I loved him and had depended on him since Graham died. He depended on me too, in ways he might not even acknowledge. And, though he was unlikely ever to say so, I knew this about him: he loved me too.

If even I, the easier one, the one with the fewer ties – these days not even a cat – had found an obstacle to my moving house before the matter had even been discussed, then how many stumbling-blocks would there turn out to be for Paul?

I was running ahead now. Fast. Too fast, as I would discover in due course. The law enabling gay men to marry, not just to enter into civil partnerships, in England and Wales had been passed by the British parliament and assented to by the Queen in the middle of last year. It came into force on March 13th of this year, and the first gay weddings took pace on the 29th of that month. That was exactly two months ago! Paul and I could marry, if we decided we wanted that, as soon as we liked. I wanted that. I just hadn't yet mentioned this to Paul.

I buttoned my thoughts away, much as, having emptied my bladder in a public toilet, I would feel obliged to button away my prick. All this would have to wait for discussion at some distant date. There was the bar of the Harrow to deal with first.

Paul returned from Cornwall and I returned from London on the same day. I went round to Paul's that very night. He had offered to cook for me, and I had offered to stay the night…

I hadn't been in his living-room for many seconds,

sharing the kind of embrace that is common to lovers everywhere when they have been separated for four days, when Paul said, 'I've got a present for you.' He took me up to the bedroom, leading me by the hand, which I always liked, and showed me two identical shirts laid out on the bed. 'Your is the smaller one,' he said as I went to pick the wrong one up. 'Simply because of my longer arms.' The shirts were of white cotton, and I thought them very cute. They were also quite distinctive, having little navy blue flashes inside collar and cuffs, and again above the breast pocket. I was more than touched. I realised exactly what Paul's purchase of them meant. And he knew that I knew, reading it clearly in the manner and intensity of my thanks.

We wore those shirts, the P and P shirts as I thought of them, when we went to the Harrow with Finbar the next day. (P and P? Peter and Paul. Keep up, please.) The three of us drove there separately. It just turned out that way. Paul and I arrived in the car park within seconds of each other and got out. We stopped and stared at our twin shirts. Said nothing. Was this a bit narcissistic? We didn't care. We knew that when we walked into the pub dressed like this there would be nothing more to say. In journalism they say that a picture is worth a thousand words.

'Sermons in stones and tongues in trees,' Shakespeare makes Jacques say in As You Like It. He said nothing about announcements in shirts. No doubt, if he'd wanted to, he would have done that.

Finbar's car drew in then: dark blue Jaguar nosing

through the gates of the pub car-park. 'Maybe you should have got a third one for him,' I said, meaning a third shirt, as we walked towards his car to greet him.

'Not sure I needed to,' said Paul as we drew close. 'Looks like he has an announcement of his own to make.'

'I see,' I said, peering through thick glass into the passenger seat. Then driver's and passenger door opened at once. Out stepped Finbar and, smiling, from the other side, came Hannah.

Finbar might enjoy a gay kiss from time to time to time. He might love to flirt with Paul and me. A feel of our cocks from time to time might turn him on. But his arrival here tonight with a triumphant-looking Hannah reminded me of what I should never have lost sight of. Finbar was fundamentally straight.

TWENTY

If the entrance we had made at the King Billy a few days earlier had given the impression that Finbar, Paul and I were a gay trio, not to same a threesome, the picture we now made as we walked into the Harrow could hardly have been more different. We looked like two couples, one straight, one gay, who were very much at ease in each other's company. The statement made by the two shirts that Paul and I were wearing could not have been made more clearly if one of us had rapped on the bar counter, called for silence and proclaimed our new-coupledom in a toastmaster-loud voice. Nobody needed to have any uncertainty about us or ask any questions; the situation was so clear. I realised now that wearing identical shirts was not only a brave idea of Paul's but also a clever one. Not even Francis made any comment, but pulled our pints, and poured Hannah's wine, with an approving smile playing about his lips.

'Exactly here was where we were sitting when we first met,' Paul told the others, gesturing down at the stools on which the four of us now actually sat.

'One day,' suggested Hannah, 'there'll be a blue plaque.'

'Did you know immediately?' Finbar asked. Paul and I looked uncertainly at him. 'I mean, was it love at first sight?'

I went first. 'It was for me,' I said quietly.

I saw Paul nod his agreement. Then, 'Ditto,' he said.

We tried to remember some of the things we had talked about. Paul brought up the memory of my plan to take Duarte to Calais for lunch.

'And Paul thought it was a bit cheapskate of me. That I ought to have been taking him to Bruges instead.'

'But in the event…' Paul began.

I finished for him. 'We didn't go. We stayed in bed.' There was general laughter.

'Know what?' Paul asked. Then, to my surprise, 'I'd like it if you took me to Calais for lunch. In Duarte's place.'

'I'd love that,' I said. Paul had a way of saying unexpected things that melted my heart.

We went to Calais a few days later, just Paul and I. We'd spent every night together in between, either at my house or at Paul's. Paul no longer tried to make his getaway before the dawn broke, and though I didn't say anything, I was very happy about it. And not only because it gave us longer together in bed.

I started to explore with Paul, very tentatively, the idea that the two of us might live together permanently. Paul was less eager to talk about this possible development than I was. And I was unsure whether – when we did occasionally refer to it – we were talking about *when* or *if.* I invented a new word especially for the purpose of this row-of-dots discussion. *Whifen.* Paul liked the word at least, so that was good. And we were a happy couple that set off from my house that Saturday morning at a quarter to eight.

We left my car at home and took Paul's. The Jaguar was fun, and did look stylish, but Paul's, running on Diesel as it did...

Dover welcomes arrivals along the A20 with a breath-taking view at the moment where the road comes over the summit of Shakespeare Cliff. There is the harbour spread out below, the white cliffs of the South Foreland stretching beyond. Ferries entering and leaving the harbour entrances seem frozen in mid-stride as it were, as if in a still photo. The sea stretches away towards the infinite sky and, if you're lucky with the weather – and today we were – the horizon is crowned with the white tiara of the cliffs of France.

'Wow,' said Paul, and rested his free hand on my thigh as we began the plunging two-mile descent from the pass into the town.

We shuffled off the gang-plank and onto the Pride of Burgundy at exactly ten o'clock. We found ourselves decanted straight into a bar. 'Put your watch on an hour,' Paul instructed me, at the same time adjusting his. 'Continental time.'

'A bit soon,' I objected. 'We're still tied to the quay.'

'Just do it,' he said. I did.

'That's better,' he said with a broad grin. 'Eleven o'clock now. Not too early for a beer.'

We drank it on the sheltered after-deck, watching the white cliffs unfurl like banners as we steadily left them behind, while the strip of white-flecked blue between them and us widened imperceptibly to twenty miles.

Long before then our destination grew large ahead of us. Calais beach and clock tower came into focus gradually. We docked in the wide harbour, looking out over the town, at the bone-white lighthouse standing stiff like a guardsman, and the line of orange-roofed houses that lay below, on the quay where the fishing boats came in.

What is it about the crossing of this narrow strait that touches us so? When we finally came to a stop and the ramp for the cars was lowered with a gentle bang, we were both moist-eyed. I didn't need to peer into Paul's eyes to realise this went for both of us. These days I simply knew.

I hadn't realised that Paul had a vertigo problem until we descended the tower of ramps that led down from our ship onto the quay. A couple of times I had to put a hand out to steady him. And he wasn't too happy when, after passport control I took him the quick way into town, over steel steps and a gantry, and across a swing-bridge between two docks.

But a lunch in France can be a wonderful smoother of ruffled feathers. We ate at the Coq d'Or in the town's most seaward square, enjoying a marrow-bone starter, a bavette steak with shallots and chips, and then a *mousse au chocolat*. It was a leisurely meal and by the time it was finished we had less than an hour remaining before we needed to head back to the port. We bought a few fancy things and wine at a mini-supermarket, and then I took Paul down to the quay where the fishing fleet tied up. I made him sit on an uncomfortable concrete block with me. We shared it in a one-cheek-on, one-cheek-off sort of way, and sat looking out through the harbour mouth, watching the ships come in and leave. 'I used to sit here with Graham,' I said. 'Just watching the sea.'

'I realised that,' said Paul. He took and lifted my hand and kissed the back of it. 'Obviously.'

A few minutes later he said, 'I'm not too happy abut the walk back across that gantry on the way to the boat. All right if we get a taxi?' Of course that was all right, and that was what we did. But still there remained another gantry to face. The one with ramps and stairs inside it that we foot passengers had to climb to get on board. Because the tide was now at its highest, this structure was at its maximum extension, and reared up beside the massive ferry – Spirit of Britain this time – as tall as a church tower.

Paul managed the climb up the corkscrew ramps. Just. But when we emerged at the top and had to set out across the flimsy gang-plank sixty feet above the water below, his internal balancing mechanism failed him. 'Darling, can you hold me?' he asked unhappily.

I wasn't unhappy. I never fulfilled a request more eagerly or with more joy. I wrapped an arm around his waist and he wrapped one of his round mine. Together we walked down the narrow ramp as if it had been the aisle of a church, and we were greeted by uncertain expressions on the faces of the reception committee of ferry crew who were there to greet us and make sure we didn't trip over the bulkhead as we came on board.

'It's like we just got married,' I said, once we'd made it to the solid deck of the ferry and unwrapped ourselves from each other's arms. 'Perhaps we'd better get used to it. Get in practice.'

'For whifen,' said Paul.

The return crossing was beautiful. The sun played on the sea and on the white cliffs on both sides, but the sea had risen with the tide and there was a slowly rocking swell. Sometimes a gentle-looking wave, no more than six feet high, would catch the ship a glancing sideways blow. We would hear, rising from the echoing chambers below us, the loud and melancholy bang of its strike, and feel the sudden shudder of the whole ship, this massive modern vessel, enter among our bones as if it had been a punch landed on the jaw. Then we would be silent for a moment as we contemplated the enormous, frightening power of simple, elemental things: things that were beyond human control.

Our drive home across the Romney Marsh took us

past the Harrow, just two miles from my front door. 'Fancy stopping off for one?' I said. Paul, decelerating immediately and signalling left, clearly did.

We had set out this morning wearing, once again, our matching white shirts with the blue trim, our P and P shirts, without thinking much about it. We hadn't looked as far ahead as an early evening drink at the Harrow. But now our twin-pack entrance made almost as much of an impression as it had done the first time, five days before. There were some chuckles among the nods and hallos, but they were all friendly ones.

We sat on our bar stools and ordered pints of Hophead. After even just a few hours in France this seemed a slightly strange thing to do. The beer seemed to taste different, and as for having to pay for our drinks before we touched them...

Paul said suddenly, 'Oh no.' His attention had been caught by a group of middle-aged people sitting around a table. They gave the impression of being engaged in some kind of meeting, or a post-meeting drink. They might have been the parish council, or parochial church council, or something of that sort.

'What's the matter?' I asked.

'I've just seen someone,' he said. From the sound of his voice I inferred it hadn't been a happy sight.

I scanned the group seated at the table. They all looked quite unthreatening; they actually looked as though they might all be nice. 'Which one?' I asked.

He said, 'My ex-wife.'

'Your ex-partner,' I clarified. They had split up as recently as Christmas. I remember Paul had told me I'd served them drinks and waited their table at the King Billy on the night of their split.

'No,' Paul said. 'Not Katie. I do mean my ex-wife. I once told you I'd been married briefly in my twenties.' Yes, he had told me, but he hadn't referred to that part of his life since, and I'd almost forgotten about it. He went on. 'It's Debbie. I haven't seen her in over twenty years, but you can't forget a wife.'

I found myself wondering what the etiquette of this situation was. Would they greet each other with a discreet wave? Ignore each other completely? Would one of them walk over and initiate a chat? Would I be introduced?

You couldn't forget a husband either, it was now clear. One of the women at the table, lean and with a finely sculpted face, was staring at Paul and me with undisguised astonishment.

Paul chose to ignore her. He went on drinking his Hophead with the kind of grim determination that must have been summoned by Socrates when he downed his final hemlock draught. I tried to find, not always successfully, other things to talk about.

The meeting or whatever it was that Paul's ex-wife was a part of broke up. They all stood, then stayed chatting for ages before moving off towards the door. At last they did move, and I saw Paul studiously avoiding looking at them too deliberately. He had clearly decided that if one of them made a move towards a contact it would not be him.

Paul's ex-wife and her – I presumed – husband, seemed to be hanging back. They were the last pair to move towards the door. At the last moment the woman – Debbie, Paul had called her – said something to her husband. In view of what then happened it was along the lines of, 'See you at the car,' as the man went out of the door, closing it behind him, while Debbie walked towards us. If she was Paul's age she was approaching fifty. For a woman of that age she looked amazing. When in her twenties... Well, I could only imagine how stunning she must have looked.

She smiled a greeting. It was a little forced, though. I smiled bravely back at her; I didn't dare to look at whatever expression might be inhabiting Paul's face.

'You both look very cosy,' she said. 'Matching shirts and all. Very cute.'

I felt a minor twinge of relief. Maybe we were going to get off lightly, I thought.

'Debbie, this is Peter.' Paul introduced us and, rather, stiffly, we shook hands.

Debbie turned her fine face towards me. I saw great strength of character in it. 'No doubt Paul has told you: I'm his wife.'

'Ummm...?' I wasn't going to be so rude as to correct her slip with the word, *ex-wife*.

Paul said, 'Debbie, no. Please.' I was disconcerted to hear desperation in his voice.

Debbie took no notice of Paul. She continued to look at me. 'Perhaps he said, ex-wife. Which isn't quite the truth. But that's a detail. You need to know, more importantly, that Paul won't stay with you. He's good at promises and long on charm, but he won't stay the course. He never can.'

Paul seemed too flattened to stand up for himself, but sat slumped and frozen on his stool. Though I too had been stunned by what Debbie had said about still being married to him, I managed to come to his defence. 'That isn't true, Debbie. He was with his last female partner for twenty years. I don't know whether you knew that already. It does suggest a degree of staying power.'

It seemed that Debbie had one of the most useful attributes there is for getting on in the world: the ability to ignore the last thing that has been said to you if it isn't convenient to reply to it. 'His first fling with a boy lasted six months, no more.'

Paul said something at last. 'It wasn't a boy. He was eighteen.'

'It was illegal at the time,' said Debbie. 'And you were twenty-seven.'

She turned back to me. 'It was the reason for our

break-up. But of course it couldn't last. It never can.'

I felt myself turn hot and cold by turns. To be spoken to in this way by a stranger was bad enough, but it was becoming far worse because the ground was shifting under me. I no longer knew who Paul was. I knew nothing about Paul.

I tried bravely. 'If you're saying that gay relationships can't last, then you're absurdly wrong.' I tried to soften this by smiling at Debbie then, but no smile came back from her, so I switched mine off. I said, a bit more toughly, 'A generation ago people may have thought like that, but things are different now. These days everyone's heard of gay couples, probably including a few among their friends, who've been together twenty, thirty years and more.'

'Lived together, yes,' said Debbie. 'Been totally faithful to each other like husband and wife, I suggest no.'

'Come on,' I said. 'You can't possibly know. I had a twenty-year relationship with a man called Graham. We remained in love throughout that time, and it only ended because he died.' I paused for a second, to give her the chance to say a polite I'm sorry, but she didn't seize the opportunity.

She said, 'Look me in the eyes and tell me you were a hundred percent faithful all that time.' She paused a nano-second then re-attacked. 'There, I'm right. You can't do it.'

I was starting to hate this woman. Paul said, 'You can't ask that. Nobody can. Not to someone in a heterosexual relationship. Not to someone who's gay. You've said your piece, Debbie. Now would you mind leaving us alone? I'd rather like you to go.' His words were polite, but the way he spat them out suggested that he was not far from getting off his stool and physically putting her out of the door.

'I'm going,' Debbie said. 'My partner's waiting in the car.' But she had one more missile to fire before she turned away. 'Look at you two. Peas in a pod sitting there, smug as all get out in your matching clothes. You're like a couple of kids. All you people are. You never grow up. You can't. You don't know how.' Then at last she turned away and walked to the door.

The silence that followed her exit was intense. At last the other people in the pub began to talk again, carefully avoiding looking at Paul and me. Between the two of us the silence continued a few seconds longer. I broke it. With an ill-judged cliché. 'Hell hath no fury like a woman scorned,' I said.

'Shut it,' said Paul.

'What?' I said, astonished, and now too hurt to think.

Then Paul leaned, almost fell towards me. He put one arm around my shoulder and laid his cheek against mine. I felt his silent sobs convulse his frame as, futilely, he tried to suppress the sorrows of the entire world as they crowded in on him now all at once.

TWENTY-ONE

It was a silent drive back to my house. At least we were together, and I laid a hand supportively on Paul's knee as he drove.

We had bought a baguette and some charcuterie in Calais for an evening snack. We ate very little of it. We talked of nothing very much, and drank very little of the wine we had brought back. Paul was clearly in a state of shock. I didn't press him to explain things. I thought I'd give him time. Yet I was in a state of shock too. I needed to know some things. OK, he was still married to someone else. OK, he'd had a six-month affair with a teenager when he was in his late twenties. I could cope with those things. But he had revealed a minor episode from his past when we'd been in Portugal with Finbar, yet had withheld these major things. Would he have told me eventually, choosing his moment carefully, had Debbie not appeared out of the blue? Or not? In which case, what else had he kept hidden from me? I was going to share a bed tonight with the man I loved, but he was also a man of secrets, a man I didn't know.

At last, when we were lying in bed together, naked and side by side, I cracked. Up to a point. 'Do you want to tell me anything about it?' I said. 'I'll still love you, whatever you have to say.'

'I don't want to talk about it,' he said.

'OK,' I said, trying to be OK. 'I'm fine with that.' I

was trying very hard to be fine with that. 'Maybe another day.'

He grunted in reply.

I reached out with my hand and grasped his slack cock. I stroked it for a moment, but then he gently picked my hand up and put it back on me, like someone removing the pick-up arm from a vinyl disc. He said, 'If you want to knock one out yourself, feel free.'

'Thank you,' I said. 'I probably won't.'

We lay awake for most of that night, flat on our backs, not speaking, not touching. I know that I was awake, of course: my thoughts were in a tempest, my heart in near-despair. I could tell from Paul's breathing that he was awake too…

I must have gone to sleep at some point. Dawn was breaking and suddenly Paul wasn't beside me. I leapt out of bed and rushed round the house naked calling his name like a lost child. I looked out at the garden. The driveway held the information I was looking for. Paul's car wasn't there.

I went back upstairs. His clothes had all gone from the bedroom chair. Including his P and P shirt, the white shirt with the blue trim that was the same as mine. Its absence was a weird sort of consolation. At least he hadn't abandoned it as well as me.

I phoned him. His mobile was switched off. His landline went to message after a few rings. I wasn't up to composing a message. I texted him. *It's fine if you don't want to talk. Just be with me.* And the usual expression of love, and a row of x's that went on rather a lot.

I gave him two hours to answer that. Perhaps I shouldn't have left it so long. But it was still only half past seven when I drove to his house. His car wasn't outside. That didn't stop me knocking loudly at the back and front doors, and peering through windows while I tapped on those as well.

I tried his mobile once again. Still switched off. My text to him, still unanswered, stared impotently out of the screen at me. I really did not know what to do. I went back to my car and got into the driver's seat, as if it was some equivalent of a thinking-cap, and might help me come up with an idea.

When I lost Graham I had Finbar to help me through. When Portia was killed I had Paul to run to. Now I had lost Paul as well, and I didn't have anywhere to go. I sat in the car for over an hour, while along the nearby road other cars took children to school and adults to work, just as if it had been an ordinary day: one on which the world hadn't come to a sudden end.

Eventually I phoned Finbar. 'Could you find time for a chat later today?' I asked him.

'It's Paul, isn't it,' he said. 'Something's happened with Paul.'

'He's gone somewhere and I don't know where....'

He cut me off. 'Come in to mine at seven. No, on second thoughts I'll come to you. In case Paul decides to show. I'm sorry it can't be sooner. Are you sure you're OK?'

I'd held it together till he asked that, but hearing his voice so caring and tender now made me start to cry. I said, 'I'll be OK when I see you.'

'Hang in there till then,' he said. 'Now I must go. My other hand's inside a cow.'

Finbar phoned me twice in the course of that never-ending day, and I phoned Paul more often than that. But nothing came back from Paul. I'd even have been happy if Paul had first got in touch with Finbar rather than me. How quickly does self-esteem disintegrate, and the threshold of what you'll settle for come down low.

A few days ago Paul and I had changed our duvet cover together. A few days before that we had changed his. We'd both said the obvious. 'First time changing the duvet with someone else since...' We'd both had a year of changing the duvet on our own. Did we want to go back to that? I knew I didn't.

Paul had said, 'It will hurt. Love always does.' It was hurting for me now. For him too? I had no doubt about that.

Soul-baring conversations with Finbar that Paul had said he'd had? What had they been about? I didn't care now. Whose cock had he sucked red wine off? I no longer cared about that either. There was nothing I could have cared about less. I just wanted my Paul back.

Finbar rang my doorbell on the dot of seven. He was clutching two bottles of red wine. 'I thought we might need them both,' he said.

I said, 'Hmm. I've already opened two. They're breathing by the fire.'

'We can see how it goes,' said Finbar casually. Then, still clutching his two bottles, he put his arms around me and hugged me fiercely and protectively.

In a way it was like it had been during the year between Graham's death and my falling in love with Paul. When Finbar would come round to my house, or I'd go to his, at least one evening a week, and we'd chew the fat over a bottle of red or two. And yet it wasn't the way it had used to be; it couldn't be again. The advent of Paul had changed everything even if, ironically, it was Paul who had brought me closer, especially in a sexual way, to Finbar.

By the time we'd sat down with a glass in front of each of us and Finbar, lounging back in his armchair, jeans-clad legs spread in front of him, said, 'Tell me all about it,' I was more than prepared. I'd had all day to think about what I was going to say, to put my thoughts and feelings into some sort of order in the process, and to polish the result as carefully as if I were going to make an award acceptance speech.

Finbar heard me to the end without interrupting. I told him about the wonderful day we'd had in France, and about the dire consequences of our chance encounter with Debbie in the Harrow. 'She claims they're still married,' I told Finbar. 'And Paul hasn't told me that's untrue. He hasn't told me it's true either. So I don't know what to think. The next thing is that she claims he ran off with a teenage boy while they were together, that the affair lasted six months and that ultimately she and Paul broke up because of it. He doesn't deny that either, and seems to accept it's true. He made a point of arguing that the kid, who was eighteen apparently, would have been legal if it had happened more recently. But later he was totally silent on both subjects, refused to open up when I gently asked him to, then he left me while I was asleep in bed with him.'

'At least you'd gone to bed in the same bed,' Paul finally said. 'Hold onto that.'

'I will,' I said. 'There's another thing I'm holding onto. He went off this morning wearing his white, blue-trimmed shirt. At least I presume he was wearing it, since he didn't leave it behind.'

Finbar nodded seriously. He saw the significance of this. 'Had he wanted to show that he was rejecting you the simplest thing would have been to leave it behind. Like throwing it in your face.' I nodded. 'Then you're almost home and dry,' Finbar said, startling me. 'He doesn't reject you. He still wants you, and he's got the shirt to prove it.'

For a moment I was radiant with hope again, but almost at once I was down in the depths again. I said, 'Unless he chucked it in the road as a symbolic gesture, or buried it like a dead cat.'

'Oh don't be silly,' said Finbar. 'You know Paul better than that. Anyway, he isn't a woman, he's a bloke.'

'Thank you,' I said. 'And thank you for listening to all of that.'

Finbar smiled. 'That was the easy bit.' He topped my glass up. 'Now tell me what the problem is.'

'The problem? What do you mean? Bloody hell!' Was Finbar not taking this seriously after all?

'I just think we should think about what it is we're trying to find a solution to, that's all,' he said. 'Sorry if I put that the wrong way. But listen: he told us both back in Portugal that he'd had one gay experience and you seemed fine with that. Now you've learned he had another one – even if it seems to have been a bit more serious... Look, Peter, it was a very long time ago. It doesn't touch him and you.'

'Yeah,' I said uncertainly, 'but then, why couldn't he have told me about such a major thing? We've had three months of sharing confidences.'

Finbar raised his hand an inch or two. 'Come back to that later, can we? Next thing: he hasn't got a divorce from his first wife. For whatever reason. It was also a long time ago. You haven't married him. He hasn't committed bigamy. Thousands of people deal with living with someone they can't marry because they're already married to someone else. Is that a special problem for you?'

'Hmm,' I said. I didn't feel strong enough to admit to Finbar that I'd had dreams of getting officially married to Paul one day.

'Well then,' said Finbar. 'We've taken Occam's razor to those little issues. Now you tell me what the real problem is.' He gave me a supportive smile.

Bless Finbar! I'd never loved him more. He'd made me see it clearly. Allowed me to see the wood by cutting down the trees. 'OK' I said. 'The problem is that he has left me and I don't know where to find him. And that I don't know him any more. When he's kept so much hidden... I don't know if I can trust him now.'

'Then the solution is simple,' said Paul. 'We have to track him down and find out where he is. Then you must go and see him and find out if he's the person you thought he was.' He shrugged. 'You might find out that he isn't. But I know him a little now. And I'd lay a hefty bet you were right about him on day one, and that what you saw then is what you've got now. It's just that it may take him a while to sort out what he wants to say to you.'

I stood up then and was going to cross the room, lift Finbar out of his chair and give him a kiss, or at least a hug. But I was prevented from doing that by the sudden ringing of the doorbell.

'That'll be Hannah,' Finbar said calmly. 'I said she should come round and join us. Hope that's OK.'

TWENTY-TWO

It wasn't OK, though I could hardly say so. I had got into a sort of *Finbar and me against the world* mode in the last hour. It was where I'd been in the dark days before I had met Paul. Now, armed with my new knowledge that Finbar did have a bit of a gay side, even if it was only a small bit of one, I had started to think during the second or third glass of wine that if the damage done between Paul and me was irreparable and I could never get my new love back, then I might have a stab at trying for Finbar instead.

Hannah's cheerful arrival in the hallway and the kiss with which she greeted Finbar put paid to that little wine-dream at once.

My discomfited state didn't last long, though. Hannah's ever-positive attitude and sunny temperament soon infected both Finbar and myself, and I found myself thinking that it was more than OK that Finbar had wanted Hannah to come along tonight. It was more than OK if the two of them became an item. I wanted Paul more than I wanted Finbar, love Finbar deeply though I did. I *would* find Paul. I *would* get him back.

The three of us talked and talked. Went round in circles, it has to be said. Finbar had already put his finger on the nub of the Paul and me situation before Hannah had got here, and we were spending a lot of the time speculating uselessly on where Paul might have gone to and what he might be doing there. It was nice, though, sitting in front of the log fire…

My phone burped suddenly in my pocket. It was nearly midnight and someone had sent me a text. The others looked at me full of expectation as I got the phone out and looked at it. I saw, as if in a dream, the words: *Had to go to Almería on business. Will be in touch.* My eyes had already gone ahead to the next and last bit: *xxxxxxxx*

'Well,' said Finbar gently, watching me. 'No doubt *who* that was. Want to tell us *what?*'

I looked at Finbar. His image had gone misty in the second since I'd last looked at it. 'He loves me,' I said.

I was up most of the rest of that night. Trying to find a flight to Almería. Everything was solidly booked. I couldn't quite believe that, till I googled the city's information pages and found a golfing event was in full … er … swing in the region over the next few days. I'd never remotely wanted to go to Almería before, but now, the night that my future happiness depended on it…

I would have to fly to Málaga and take a bus along the coast, or else a train via Granada on an inland route. It took me quite some time to find all this out. I decided to go to Málaga anyway and decide then about my next steps. I booked a flight that left Gatwick around eleven o'clock. That meant no going to bed tonight. I'd need to be on the road in a couple of hours. Even so, I wouldn't get to Almería before evening. I wanted to be there now, afraid that Paul would slip through my fingers like sand or water.

I looked at my watch. It was four a.m. and the birds were starting to wake outside in the pale morning light. I emailed Paul. He always checked his emails as soon as he got up. Even so, he wouldn't be reading this for a few hours yet. Nevertheless…

My Darling

I'm flying to join you in Almería. Coming via Málaga, and will be with you tonight. There's things I need to say even if you don't want to talk. I'll say the main ones now, though. I love you with all my heart, and, because of that, there's nothing that can go wrong between us – even if things go terribly wrong – that can not be put right.

I added my name and a large number of x's. I won't spell them all out…

I packed enough stuff for a few nights, showered and got dressed. For better or worse I put on my P and P shirt. Then I drove off into the early morning of this momentous day, trying, as I left the driveway, not to wake Finbar and Hannah, or my other neighbours, up.

'Date of return?' they asked me when I went for my ticket at the airport car-park.

'I've really no idea,' I said. 'What do you suggest?'

I had already checked in when an email landed on my phone. From Paul of course.

Darling

I don't think it's a good idea for you to come all the way out here. Though yes, I'm prepared to talk when I get back. Thing is, though, I don't think we can go on with our relationship. You're a very straightforward guy and I am not. This would cause problems down the line, and you would get hurt. Better if we end it now, I think.

We'll always be friends. But let's leave it like that, while the memories are good.

With love or what you will

Paul xxx

I replied at once.

My Dearest Darling Paul

Bollocks to that. I'm already through security at Gatwick and my flight to Málaga will be called in a few minutes. I'll call you when I arrive at Málaga and we can arrange when and where to meet.

Longing to see you.

Pete xxxxxxxxxxxxxxxx

There was no reply to that before the time came for boarding, and as soon as I got on the plane I turned my phone firmly off.

Málaga was full of June warmth and the sky was shrill with swifts. Crowns of jacaranda trees made it even bluer than it was. I switched my phone back on with a bit of trepidation, bracing myself. There was a text.

You win, for the moment. Ring when you touch down and I'll know where we can meet. xxxxx

I counted the number of x's twice. The less you have to go on the more you try to read into what little there is. Like when the Bible was the only book. So I nibbled away at Paul's unusual phrase: I'll *know* where we can meet. That meant, I supposed, that at the time of writing he did not know. For whatever reason. There was a very easy way to find out. At least it would be easy if Paul picked up...

He did. We had a very businesslike conversation. About logistics. He would be finished with his dealings in Almería in another hour at the most. We could meet in Granada, roughly equidistant from Almería and Málaga, and stay there the night. If we both took trains we could meet at the station...

My train wound up from the coast through rocky gorges, crossed a flat plain, and then made its way up a steady incline among mountains that grew in stature the more we climbed. At last I was faced with mountain tops I'd last seen from a plane window – Mulhacen and the Sierra Nevada, veiled and gowned with snowy lace.

As it happened the train would continue to Almería after it had dropped me off. Trotting along the display panel went the names of the stations it would be calling at. Even now Paul was making his way along the same list as slowly our paths converged and the distance between us grew less. Guadix, Moreda, Iznalloz. They sounded like place-names, or characters, in The Lord of the Rings. I found myself wondering how you pronounced Iznalloz… Ithnaloth, I guessed. Perhaps, by the time I met him, Paul would know this.

He didn't smile when he saw me coming into the station concourse from the platform among a crowd. Nor did his face light up at once, although it usually did. 'Have you been to Granada before?' he asked after we'd had a perfunctory kiss.

'No,' I said.

And then he smiled. 'Then let me show you it.'

So I smiled too – realising as I did so that I too had failed to smile before this moment. Of course it would be lovely to be shown this fabled place by Paul. It would give a purpose to our being here together that was more enjoyable than the prospect of a heavy talk. After all, what man of forty-eight looks forward to explaining why he failed to get divorced in his late twenties, or what made him run off with a teenage boy around the same time and then fail to tell you about it?

The city laid its spell on us very quickly. 'I booked us a hotel in the grounds of the Alhambra Palace,' Paul said casually, as the taxi he hailed for us outside the station threaded its upward way through a tissue of narrow streets.

We sat in the back of the taxi and I could feel the warm pressure of Paul's hip-bone against mine. He made no attempt to push his knee against mine, though, and I took my cue from him and didn't try to press mine against his. And, as we were in the back of a taxi and in full view of the driver's mirror, we made no attempt to stroke each other's crotch or inner thigh.

The Hotel America didn't have roses round the door, it had crimson bougainvillea instead. It was an old building, set in the main 'street' of the Alhambra proper, snug inside the great Moorish walls, midway between the lower palaces and the Generalife on its garden height. Our room was beamed and characterful. It was wonderful in fact. The bathroom was clad from floor to waist-height with Moorish azulejo tiles, and its panelled door of chestnut had a hatch set into it at head height that you could open and look in at your companion through, while he or she sat on the loo. We got just as far as taking our coats off before I said, 'I haven't had a hug yet, Paul. We're in the Alhambra, you know.'

Paul wrapped himself around me then, whether he'd been thinking of doing so a moment earlier or whether he had not. And in the middle of our long embrace in which all the pent-up pain and hurt and longing of two days came pouring out I found that, despite Paul's greater height and strength it was the easiest thing ever to topple him onto the double bed...

Afterwards we at last unpacked a bit and hung our coats up. Our room had a walk-in hanging-cupboard nesting among the beams, and we walked into it, larking about in there, like the children in The Lion, the Witch and the Wardrobe, among the coats. I mentioned this. 'Can't promise you a witch,' Paul said. 'But lions I can offer. When we get inside the palace itself.' We went down to reception. We were too late for a visit to the palace that evening, they told us; we booked for a visit the next morning instead.

We walked into town. *We walked into town.* Sounds too ordinary. I need to elaborate on that. We strolled down the street of the Alhambra, inside the walls, past the monumental extension to the palace that was built by Charles V, and exited our protected enclave through a massive 14th century gate. The Gate of Justice bears two emblems engraved in the stone above its lofty Moorish entrance arch. One is a hand, the other a key. On the day the hand reached down from among the stones and seized the key, so the legend went, the Alhambra would fall to the Christian kings of Spain. The Alhambra did fall. In 1492, while Columbus sailed the ocean blue, and great was the fall of it. The hand moved not at all, though. At least, it was still fixed in its place the night we walked beneath it.

From there our way led down a sandy pathway through Sleeping Beauty chestnut woods in which old iron lamp-posts were set about. 'First the wardrobe,' I had to say. 'Now this.'

And then, as our sandy path gave way to the ancient street the Cuesta de Gomérez, we did begin to talk. Neither of us forced ourselves or forced the other: it just naturally came out.

TWENTY-THREE

I said, 'Nothing's happened that we need to split up over. You need to know that.' We were passing a guitar maker's shop on the steep slope down. Music was playing inside the lighted window. We almost pressed our noses against the glass. The guitarero was closing up, putting his half-finished instruments away. The flamenco we heard was coming from a CD. It was good enough.

We were still facing in through the bright glass when Paul said, 'I spent a lot of time insisting I was straight before I met you. Well, thanks to Debbie you've found out that wasn't true.'

'You'd simplified things a bit,' I said. We both continued to stare ahead of us through the glass at spoke-shaves and cramps and moulding-planes, and guitars of slightly different colours, amber through cherry to chestnut, hanging in rows the way the haunches of jamon serrano hang from the ceiling in Spanish bars.

'I was lying to you,' said Paul.

'If you want to put it like that... OK then, I absolve you from your sin. *Ego te absolvo.*' I thought for a moment. 'The only consequence of that is that I can no longer congratulate myself on being the one who turned you. Perhaps that's a good thing.'

'A good thing?'

'I mean, to have my vanity pricked.'

Paul swung away from the shop window towards me. He bunged his arms around me. 'Don't think like that.' His voice came raw and rough. 'You're the first man I've fallen head-over-heels in love with in such a big way. That tells you everything you need to know about yourself. It's a bigger achievement than "turning me" as you put it. Be proud of that if you can be. *If* you can, *whifen* you can, it's bigger and better than just vanity.'

I said, 'So we're not splitting up then?'

'No, we're fucking not.' The words came loud in the Spanish street, They came like the bang of a great wave against the hull of the small ship that was me. Jawbone smack.

I said, 'Tell me about the boy.'

We had come to the bottom of the Cuesta de Gomérez and almost literally fallen out of it into the Plaza Nueva, among the countless cafés with their tables out on the pavements of the square. We selected one at random, sat down and ordered a beer each. By the time Paul finished his tale we had got through four...

Paul's father was a stockbroker. He had had the luck

to make a killing early in life and, adding those proceeds to a substantial inheritance from his own father, had moved out of London into the Sussex countryside while investing most of his fortune in the Cornish and overseas properties that had now become Paul's.

Paul, who had been earmarked for university by his parents, had given them the finger by training as a carpenter instead. But they had had the last laugh: Paul became his father's maintenance man. Soon he did additional courses in plumbing and electrics. He even had the paperwork to prove that he was legally entitled to install not only an electric oven but also a gas boiler and a gas fire. His father worked him hard; Paul was already married by the time his father agreed to get him an assistant. An eighteen-year-old boy called Sol.

'Sol?' I queried at that point. 'As in, Latin for the sun?'

'No. Short for Solomon. But unusual all the same.'

At that time Paul was straight as a dye – or so he would have said. OK, there had been a few exploratory fumbles in his childhood and teens. Mutual inspection of equipment behind the bike sheds. Nothing amounting to anything as affirming as a wank. But straight was how Paul saw himself. Straight was what he wanted to be.

'Like all of us at that age,' I said. 'Like me.'

Paul smiled.

Paul working in close physical proximity to Sol...

Well, it wasn't hard to guess how things had gone. A trip to Almería together. Drinks. Dinner. More drinks. Sharing a hotel room... It turned out that Sol, country boy that he was, had never taken much of an interest in girls... A full-blown affair developed. Sol was extremely handsome, Paul told me. He gave me one of those lopsided grins I hadn't seen for days. 'He was your size,' he said. 'And shape. Nice cock, like yours.'

'Thank you,' I said.

'Though not quite as big.'

'Aww...'

'I left my wife for him.' The words came stark and sudden after the banter. We were on our third beer by now. 'It didn't work out. Trips abroad together were one thing. In England, though, where would we live? We got a shabby flat in Hastings. His parents were beside themselves. My father was furious with me. He sacked Sol. The pressure got too much for Sol. After six months with me he walked out. We saw each other from time to time. We never got back together.'

'My poor darling,' I said. It was an expression I'd never used before. Not even with Graham. It just came out.

Paul had taken the plunge. He had leapt from one branch to another, hopeful of everything, and the branch he had landed on broke. Call me sentimental but I now put my hand across his, over the table top and said, 'I'll never let you down.'

He said, 'I should bloody well hope you won't.'

After all this I now had the painful duty of asking him how it had come about that his wife from more than twenty years before was still married to him.

'She was brought up a strict Catholic,' Paul said. 'Her family wouldn't countenance divorce.'

I said, 'But she lives with a man. At least, that was the impression I got. How does her family square that?'

'Fair question,' said Paul. 'Living in sin, perhaps, they'd call it. Anyway, no business of mine. They live at the other end of the county. Our bad luck they ended up in the Harrow that night. Were they at some sort of reunion, do you think?'

Was it bad luck? I wondered. It had helped us get some things into the open. Helped us to get to know each other better. Well, it had helped me to get to know Paul better at any rate. Where I was concerned there was still something...

I put it to one side. I said, 'It makes no difference to me that you're still married. We've never talked of getting married ourselves. I've never given it a thought.'

Paul looked at me searchingly, but there was also amusement in his look. 'Oh, but I think you had.'

'No, honestly,' I fibbed.

Paul made a clucking, chuckling noise in his throat. 'Sometimes you forget I am your alter ego, Peter. I read you like a book.'

'In which case,' I said, 'Let me put it on record. I no longer care about getting married officially. I'll be happy to live in sin with you for the rest of my life. To dedicate the rest of my life to you from this day forward. If you'll have me, that is.' I stopped.

'Why wouldn't I have you?' I felt the weight of Paul's hand descending on my knee underneath the table as he said this.

'Perhaps there's something I ought to have told you,' I said.

'Hmm,' said Paul. There had been a look of something like joy on his face a moment ago. Now there was a thoughtful frown. 'Perhaps we should look for something to eat before you do.'

We didn't have to look far. Paul knew an old and famous drinking haunt just off the Plaza Nueva. It was called the Castañeda, or chestnut tree. It did good food, Paul said, as we paused outside. We pushed the door open and went inside. It was full of old beams and barrels and a glowing, welcoming yellowish light: it was the kind of Spanish bar I loved. I waited till we'd drunk a manzanilla and had got stuck into plates of wind-dried cod with a comforting bottle of Rioja to accompany before I embarked on my tale.

'You've come clean with me about your eighteen-year-old,' I said. 'I guess I'd better tell you about mine.'

'Only if you want to,' said Paul.

'He wasn't eighteen, though,' I said. 'He was just sixteen.'

'That too would be legal now,' Paul reminded me gently.

'It wasn't then.' I drew a breath. 'I'd just left drama school. Age twenty-one. I'd been fucked a few times. Smallish, cute-ish: that's what happens.' Paul nodded slowly. He was still cute, but had probably never been small. 'My first acting job was on a tour. An Alan Ayckbourn play. We spent a week in Bristol. OK, we spent a week everywhere. But this happened in Bristol. There was a party one night, given by the local playgoers' club. There was this kid – OK, sixteen-year-old – who was very into us young actors. It got late and he stayed and stayed. Finally the theatre staff made closing-up noises and we were out in the autumn air. I ended up on the pavement alone with this lad – his name was Russell, by the way – and I said to him, "Where's your home?" I was getting a bit concerned for him by now. He said, "My parents'll have locked up and gone to bed by now. They don't mind me being out at night. Can I come back to yours?"

'That was all a bit of a shock: all three bits of it. But I said – well of course I did – "OK, come on then; my digs are just a few hundred yards from here." As it happened, I had a studio flat for the week; not a room in someone's house, thankfully. We walked together. When we got there I said, "There's just one bed, I'm afraid. You can share it with me or have the floor." He said, "I'll share with you."

'He stripped naked even quicker than I did. He was small and scrawny but his cock was massive. He pulled on it a bit while we stood beside the bed. Then he said, "It doesn't come, if that's what you're thinking about. It never has. I like being fucked actually."

'He was sixteen, I was twenty-one, but it seemed he had more sexual experience than me. I was suddenly determined to catch up. I was also completely hard. I pulled him into bed and he turned his arse towards me. I'd never done this to anyone but that night I fucked another person for the very first time. I pulled his cock as well. He liked that a lot but, as he'd warned me, nothing came out of it. He enjoyed being fucked much more. My cock was still embedded in him when we went to sleep.

'We were woken by the noise of his father banging on the door. We were both terrified. I pulled on some jeans and a pullover and went downstairs. "D'you have my son?" the father shouted at me.

'I said, "He stayed the night on my floor. He stayed too late at the party and didn't think he'd be able to get home."

'I was ready to crap myself, but the father took it on board and nodded and said, "He does that sometimes. I'm sorry you were inconvenienced." Then he called his son's name and Russell, now fully dressed, came down.

They left together.'

'And?' asked Paul. 'You broke the law, OK. By today's standards you did nothing wrong, though.'

'I saw him again,' I said. 'He came down to where I shared a flat in London. We had sex together several more times…'

'And?' asked Paul again. 'Were you with Graham at the time?'

'No,' I said.

'Even if you had been,' Paul said, 'who would I be to cast stones?' He gave me a look of astonishment. 'Why would you imagine I might be shocked, or might not understand?'

'I don't know,' I said. I felt a bit deflated. 'I guess I just wanted to level up the playing field. I mean after what you told me…'

'Thank you for sharing,' Paul said. 'But I wasn't going to have a problem with that.'

'Then you need to know: there was no way I was going to have a problem with what you told me.'

'So have we cleared the air?' Paul asked. 'Shared our closet skeletons?'

'Yes,' I said. 'No more secrets between us from now on. OK?'

'OK,' said Paul. 'But can we also agree that we don't have to dredge our memories for every single detail we might still have buried there?'

'It's a deal,' I said. We raised our glasses and clinked them, and then I saw Paul smiling at me across the table. I had never seen such a love-lit smile on his, or anyone else's, face before. Always excepting Graham's, of course. I smiled back at him. God knows what he read into that smile of mine.

We walked back up the Cuesta de Gomérez. The guitarero's shop was closed and dark now. The uphill street ended at the Romanesque arch beyond which it turned once again into the sandy path down which we'd come. On the further side of the arch the woods started. There was the first of the lamp-posts, beckoning us onward, uphill and ahead. Together we climbed the wooded slope beneath the Alhambra walls. And as we climbed, more and more lamps began to shine out among the trees below, until the dark valley seemed studded by the reflections of the stars above.

We stopped and looked down over the handrail at that sight: dark trees below, lit up as if by glow-worms in the night. I said, 'What I told you just now – you're not quite the first person I've ever told. I told Graham...' I hesitated. 'And Finbar knew about it.'

'Of course,' said Paul. 'I'm fine with that.' Then he paused. 'Actually, I told Finbar about Sol. Hope you're

OK with that.'

You told Finbar before you told me, I thought, but I let the thought pass. 'You mentioned soul-baring conversations late at night. I did wonder what they'd been about. Anyway,' I changed the subject slightly, 'at least I know now whose cock it was you licked the red wine off.'

'Actually, no,' said Paul. 'That was someone else.' Before I could ask him, *who the fuck was that?* he had gone on smoothly, 'Are you still in love with Finbar?'

I had to think for a second. I had to be truthful, and get this right. I said, 'No. Not now. Although I was for a time. I still love him, though. Love him very much.'

'He said you were in love with him.'

I felt myself go hot. 'He told you that?'

'It's OK,' Paul said. 'I love him a little bit myself.'

'I wouldn't want to live too far away from him, though,' I said. 'Even now.'

'From him and Hannah, you mean.'

'How did you know that?' I asked. I hadn't told Paul about last night.

'I notice things,' Paul said.

I left it at that. And I didn't go back to the question of whose cock he had sucked wine off at some point in the past. If that was to remain one of his secrets, so be it; if he wanted to tell me one day then no doubt he would.

There were compromises we would both have to make. One was that I would have to accept that Paul was both gay and straight. He might have difficulties with that at moments in the future. So might I. But we'd survived a total of ninety-nine years between us. I guessed we could deal with that.

We made our way back into the Alhambra's walled compound through the zigzag tunnel that was the Justice Gate. Key and hand remained inviolably separate as we passed beneath. Then we walked up the now empty lane beside the palace. There were just us. Our two shadows went ahead of us on the sandy pavement. From time to time the shadows kissed. 'The witch is here,' I said.

'How do you know?' Paul asked.

'Because she is,' I said. 'You can't see her, of course, but here she is. She isn't a bad witch.'

'Not if she's here with us tonight,' said Paul. 'Tonight she's a good witch.'

I said, 'The best.'

We reached our hotel. It was in darkness. But we rang the bell and a kind young man let us in. We looked about us in the subdued light of the entrance hall. There was an equally dimly lit but somehow inviting lounge. 'Do you think we could have a coffee before we go to bed?' Paul asked the young man.

'And perhaps a coñac with it?' I said.

We had both coffee and the nightcap, sitting in the darkened lounge that had become suddenly our private sitting-room. It was furnished with old-fashioned upholstered and leather armchairs. It felt a bit like my own house.

'One day we'll have a place like this,' I said. 'Just for us.'

'This not good enough for you?' Paul asked. He reached out from his armchair to mine and took my hand.

'Hang on,' I said. 'We're not quite close enough.' I stood up, picked up the armchair I was sitting in and moved it till it was touching his. I'd never seen anyone do this in a film or in real life, or read of it happening in a book. But this night I did it. Then I sat down again, and we placed our forearms together, touching, side by side.

'One day,' I said, 'we'll go back to Tuscany.'

'Drive up to Radicofani,' Paul said.

The sound of that… I went on. 'If you're OK with it I'll show you the spot in the Brede woods where Graham's ashes are.'

Paul squeezed my hand, 'I'd be honoured,' he said. 'And I'd like you to take me to the Montreal. When you get the chance. Oh, by the way, I heard from the police in Portugal. They've got my money back.'

It sounded very unimportant just now. I said, 'I'm glad of that. Sorry, but right now it seems the least important thing in the world.'

'You're right,' said Paul, 'it is. Today matters. OK, and tomorrow.'

'Tell me about tomorrow,' I said.

'Tomorrow,' said Paul a bit sleepily, 'I shall show you the magic of the Nazrid Palace. The water basins and the myrtle hedges. The quince trees whose blossom is full of bees. The honeycomb ceilings of the Ambassadors' Hall, and the fountain stained with conspirators' blood. The lions with water spouting from their muzzles...'

'Lions and tigers and bears,' I said.

'The apartments where Washington Irving lived and wrote...'

'Then after that I'll take you home,' I said. 'I'll show you the place where we shall...'

Paul put one of his fingers to my lips. 'Whifen,' he said.

'Whifen,' I agreed. 'Meanwhile, right now I'm taking you upstairs to bed.'

'No whifen about that at least,' he said. He gave me one of his whimsical, lopsided looks. I studied his face for a moment and then I returned the look. At least I think I did. Tried to at any rate. But it's a wise man indeed who can read the expressions on his own face.

We got to our feet, said thank you and goodnight to the man at the reception desk who had made our coffee, then made our way up the stairs. Try as we might we couldn't stop the floorboards creaking as we went. Paul turned the key in the lock of the first door we came to. 'I hope I've brought us to the right place,' he said.

I said, 'I think you have.'

THE END

****

Anthony McDonald is the author of over twenty novels. He studied modern history at Durham University, then worked briefly as a musical instrument maker and as a farmhand before moving into the theatre, where he has worked in every capacity except director and electrician. He has also spent several years teaching English in Paris and London. He now lives in rural East Sussex.

Novels by Anthony McDonald

SILVER CITY

THE DOG IN THE CHAPEL

TOM & CHRISTOPHER AND THEIR KIND

RALPH: DIARY OF A GAY TEEN

IVOR'S GHOSTS

ADAM

BLUE SKY ADAM

GETTING ORLANDO

ORANGE BITTER, ORANGE SWEET

ALONG THE STARS

WOODCOCK FLIGHT

MATCHES IN THE DARK: 13 Tales of Gay Men

(Short story collection)

Gay Romance Series:

Gay Romance: A Novel

Gay Romance on Garda

Gay Romance in Majorca

The Paris Novel

Gay Romance at Oxford

Gay Romance at Cambridge

The Van Gogh Window

Gay Romance in Tartan

Tibidabo

Spring Sonata

Touching Fifty

Romance on the Orient Express

All titles are available as Kindle ebooks and as paperbacks from Amazon.

www.anthonymcdonald.co.uk

36615129R00140

Printed in Great Britain
by Amazon